The people of Windsor tolerate Eva Dohrmann because she was once wealthy and important. But lately, Eva's behavior has grown eccentric and unbearable: wearing those gaudy hats and that fur cape straight through the summer; driving the battered yet once stylish cars now stuffed with other people's junk; and her habit of strolling through local restaurants and sweeping tips right off tables. Little kids run from her; teen-agers joke about her and tell gruesome stories about her mysterious past. But for Ellen Dohrmann, Eva is no laughing matter . . . because Eva happens to be Ellen's grandmother.

Defying her mother's orders to stay away from Eva, fifteen-year-old Ellen takes her best friend, Josie, with her to investigate Eva's bizarre lifestyle and rescue her from this steady deterioration. But the terrible reality of what Eva has become hits Ellen with a shock she never expected. Now Ellen is forced to recognize Eva Dohrmann as she is today—no longer the gentle grandmother she once knew so well, but a grave responsibility that Ellen must face to redeem her own conscience . . . and to save Eva's life.

Sweet Bells Jangled Out of Tune

ALSO BY ROBIN F. BRANCATO

Don't Sit Under the Apple Tree
Something Left to Lose
Winning
Blinded by the Light
Come Alive at 505

ROBIN F. BRANCATO

Sweet Bells Jangled Out of Tune

ALFRED A. KNOPF · NEW YORK

THIS IS A BORZOI BOOK PUBLISHED BY ALFRED A. KNOPF, INC.

Copyright © 1982 by Robin F. Brancato
Jacket illustration Copyright © 1982 by Michael Garland
All rights reserved under International and Pan-American
Copyright Conventions. Published in the United States by
Alfred A. Knopf, Inc., New York, and simultaneously in Canada by
Random House of Canada Limited, Toronto.
Distributed by Random House, Inc., New York.
Manufactured in the United States of America
10 9 8 7 6 5 4 3 2 1

Library of Congress Cataloging in Publication Data
Brancato, Robin F. *Sweet bells jangled out of tune.*
Summary: Fifteen-year-old Ellen wants to do something to help
her dead father's mother, an eccentric old lady
she has been forbidden ever to speak to or visit.
[1. Grandmothers—Fiction.   2. Old age—Fiction]
I. Title.   PZ7.B73587Sw   [Fic]   81–14283
ISBN 0–394–84809–8   AACR2
ISBN 0–394–94809–2 (lib. bdg.)

My thanks to the following people who provided me
with information that was helpful in the writing of
Sweet Bells Jangled Out of Tune:
Dr. Russell Gardner, Mary Gardner, Dr. Robert Santulli,
Dr. Michael Milano; Karen Bittner, Gloria Oden,
the staff of Harbor House at St. Joseph's Hospital,
Paterson, New Jersey; Leo Wielkocz, and Millie Astmann.

R. F. B.

Sweet Bells Jangled Out of Tune

one

"How come *I* wasn't invited?" Josie's hand slides up and down the chrome handrail.

"I wish you were," Ellen says, stepping down into the stairwell of the bus. "It's just family this year. We're having dinner here at Zimmer's because Grandpa's been sick and my mother and I have to get up early tomorrow."

Josie fluffs up her hair with her fingertips. "So have a great time while I'm *working*. My job is the pits, Ellen. I'm not kidding. *Nobody's* buying our foam insulation. It rots your lungs. Listen, order champagne tonight, okay? And one for me."

Ellen laughs. "I wish."

The bus stops and the doors fly open.

Josie's bangle bracelets tinkle as she hangs over

the stairwell. "Say hi to your grandfather for me, El. See you at lunch tomorrow—Giese's at noon. Happy birthday!"

"Thanks." Getting off the bus, Ellen looks up at the window and smiles as Josie makes a face at her. Both of them wave and the bus whooshes away.

Then Ellen turns toward the Square. Most of the shops, on summer schedule, are closed for the day. The benches on the brick island are deserted. Petunias droop in their pots at the entrance to the Franklin Building.

Ellen crosses Main Avenue and heads toward Zimmer's Restaurant, the only place in the Square that looks a little bit alive, with its red and white canopy fluttering in the breeze. There are a few cars parked in the front, but her mother's isn't among them. Ellen hesitates by the huge hanging sign: ZIMMER'S, SINCE 1924. She'd rather not walk in by herself, so she cuts through the alley to the parking lot in the rear. Beneath her feet are cobblestones like the ones that covered the entire Square until a few years ago. Straight ahead she can see the top floor of the hospital rising higher than all the other buildings in Windsor, and far beyond that, up on the mountain, she can see Windsor Tower through the haze.

Coming out of the alley, she checks the lot, but as far as she can tell, her mother, Nonie, and Grandpa aren't here yet. She's just about to sit down on a bench to wait for them when Ellen suddenly spies

2

what she's always half-consciously on the lookout for—an old, beat-up maroon car. As usual, her first impulse is to think of what her mother has said and to hurry away. Her second impulse, though, is to come closer.

She swallows hard, tries to stay calm. Straightening her skirt nervously, she shoves back the strands that are always falling when she tries to twist her hair up in the back.

Meanwhile, her eyes dart from one end of the lot to the other. It's been months now, a year maybe, since she last had this chance, and the attraction is so strong that Ellen dismisses the thought that her mother is due any minute. She moves across the lot.

The car is looking much worse than the last time, she sees. The maroon paint is dull as rust, one fender is horribly dented, and the rear bumper is dragging. Once the paint was glossy on all three cars—this one and the other two almost like it that must be parked back in the driveway in East Windsor. Ellen comes closer. Her mother and Nonie will die if they catch her here. She rubs a spot on the dirty window with her fingertips and peers in at the boxes, newspapers, and objects stacked up so that the only unoccupied space is the driver's seat. Some of the things—the boxes of 78 rpm records and the broken guitar—she's seen before. Others are new to her—the arm of a mannequin, a bolt of satiny cloth, an assortment of hats.

Across the lot a horn honks, and Ellen jumps. At first she thinks it's her mother. Then she sees that it's a bunch of kids in a van, and it's obvious why they're beeping their horn. Ellen stiffens as the van veers close enough to just miss the old woman in a wide fur cape who is standing by the wire wastebasket at the far end of the lot.

The horn blasts again. Somebody yells something at the woman, and a burst of laughter follows. Then the van digs out, leaving a trail of exhaust, and the woman goes back to what she was doing. Ellen watches her reach into the garbage and haul up something that she drops into the canvas bag on her arm.

Mrs. Eva Dohrmann is the woman's name. But the whole town knows her as Eva, so Ellen has come to think of her that way, too. Hiding behind the car, Ellen observes her closely, as she's been doing for years now, whenever she gets the chance. It's a hot day in June, but that doesn't bother Eva. She's wearing her matted, half-bald fur cape, the same as always, and a hat decorated with fake berries, old blue sneakers, and chains around her neck and waist that glimmer in the last rays of sunlight. Ellen wishes she could see her face, but the distance is too great.

Now Eva is dropping something else into her bag—something to add to her junk in the car. The rumor is that she collects things so she'll be prepared when the end of the world comes. Where she

4

intends to go, and how she expects to manage all three cars at once—all this is a mystery. Lots of stories are circulated about Eva. According to one, she was once the most beautiful woman in Windsor. According to another, she's hiding something terrible in her run-down East Windsor mansion. Everybody in Windsor has an Eva story. Well, almost everybody. Ellen's mother and Nonie never mention her. Josie is the only person Ellen talks to about Eva. The two of them have gone together to look at Eva's house a few times. They've had long discussions about her, whenever Ellen sleeps over at Josie's. Josie admires Eva.

Ellen crouches. Eva is hoisting up her bag and beginning to make her way across the lot. It's the chance Ellen has waited years for. To see her close up. To speak to her. And yet, as soon as Ellen hears the soft crunch of sneakers on loose pebbles, she backs away. Her throat feels as if it's been shot through with Novocaine. No sense in staying. How can she speak, or think straight, with her mother's warnings ringing in her ears? Eva's hat appears between two parked cars in the next row, and Ellen runs, in a panic, without looking back.

While she's still standing in front of Zimmer's, catching her breath and being angry at herself, her mother and grandparents pull up in front of the canopy. Ellen helps Nonie out of the back seat, then Grandpa, who pulls her ears. "Happy birthday, Ellie!"

Her mother locks the car.

"Have you been waiting long?" Nonie asks.

"No, not really," Ellen says as they walk up the steps under the canopy.

"Anything new?" her mother asks.

"No."

"Sure there is," Grandpa says. "I'm back in circulation, and this young lady's going to have the best fifteenth birthday dinner Zimmer's has to offer."

two

"Look at that, will you? Isn't that nice!" Nonie says, and Ellen nods politely as the waitress sets a cake in front of her with flaming candles and a sputtering sparkler. On her right is her mother, on her left, Grandpa. Behind her Ellen hears two off-key voices singing "Happy Birthday to You."

She turns around to see Ben Bernhauser and another busboy who's as overweight as Ben is skinny. Her family joins in the singing, which makes her feel as if she's about eight years old.

Nonie smiles. "Take a big breath now!"

Ellen blows out all but one candle. The fat busboy laughs.

"Try again," Ben says.

Ellen blows out the last candle. "I didn't know you worked here," she says to him.

"Yup. You going to be around this summer?"

She nods. "I'm working as a volunteer again at Windsor General."

"See you around, maybe. So long." Ben rolls away the cart loaded with dirty dishes as they eat their cake.

"Was that the Bernhauser boy?" Nonie asks.

"Yes," Ellen says.

"Is that an *earring* he's wearing?"

"Yes."

"Oh my land, what next! Well, they always were an odd family."

Ellen starts to answer, but she sees that her mother has just taken out a beautifully wrapped little box from her purse.

Her mother clears her throat. "Now. Here's something we hope will help you remember this day." She places the box carefully in Ellen's palm. "We hope you'll like it, Ellen. Nonie and I went to every store in town."

Grandpa nudges her. "If I'd been there, I'd have found it right off."

"Thanks. Thanks a lot—" Ellen sees them smiling at her through the last wisps of smoke from the birthday candles. She pulls off the filagree ribbon and removes the wrapping. "It's great!" she says, holding up the ring. "I really like it! This finger?" She slips it on. "Where did you finally get it?"

"Plummer's," Nonie says. "I always swear by Plummer's."

"What's the stone?"

"An aquamarine," her mother says. "Delicate, isn't it? When we saw it, Nonie said, 'That one's Ellen!' "

"I love it. Thank you." The three of them are beaming at her. "And thanks for dinner, too. It was good."

"Good enough to last till next year?" Grandpa asks. "It'd better be. We spent all our money!" He pushes his chair back. "Excuse me, ladies. I'm off to the men's room."

"Are you all right, Frank?"

"Sure I'm all right."

Nonie, watching him go, leans over and whispers. "Is that the Zimmer who was in your class, Dorothy? The man over standing there by the cash register?"

"No," Ellen's mother says. "You're thinking of Jeffrey Zimmer."

Ellen feels herself slipping away as names of old Windsor families buzz in her ears like mosquitoes. *I saw Eva*, she feels like saying, but she doesn't.

The dining room is emptying out now. Grandpa, on his way back from the men's room, has stopped to speak to someone at the bar.

Ellen yawns.

"Wasn't that the Johnson boy?" Nonie is asking. "The one who was at West Point with Fred?"

Fred. Ellen wakes up at the sound of her father's

name. Nonie doesn't mention it very often. And when she does, it's usually in a disapproving tone, as if it's his own fault that he's dead. Ellen tries now, as always, to picture the man whose photograph is on the mantel and in the albums, but all she can remember are the photographs themselves and the things her mother has told her about their life in Georgia when Ellen was a baby. She remembers the funeral at Arlington when she was four years old. That's about all.

The subject of her father has passed, and her mother and Nonie are talking about somebody else now. From the bar Grandpa gives a signal that he'll be joining them in a minute. Ellen, examining her new ring again, puts the little box in her shoulder bag. And then, looking up, she sees Eva standing in the hall between the bar and the dining room.

Ellen sits perfectly still. Eva is about twenty feet away from her, but she doesn't seem to be aware of Ellen or anybody else. Ellen glances at her mother and Nonie, who are still chattering away, and at the hostess, who is watching nervously.

Eva comes into the main part of the dining room now, the canvas bag swinging at her side.

She's thin, is the first thing Ellen notices. And the way she used to walk—like a queen almost—that's changed. She moves cautiously toward the row of cleared tables, as if she's afraid of stumbling. The chains around her neck and waist are jangling, and

10

she's wearing an assortment of rings on her fingers, over her gloves. If only she would turn so that Ellen could see her face.

Ellen sits up. Eva is sweeping her hand across the stained cloth on the empty table for two and is putting the waitress's tip into her canvas bag. Ellen watches the bills float down. She hears the coins drop. Eva moves on to the next table and does it again. The hostess whispers to the waitress now, the waitress goes to the kitchen, and the next thing Ellen knows, the manager is there. Meanwhile, Eva is moving right along. It will only be a few minutes, Ellen realizes, until Eva circles back to their table. Her mother and Nonie are still absorbed in their conversation, and neither of them looks up until Grandpa comes back from the bar. He arrives at the table just as Eva does.

Nonie draws her hand to her throat and makes a noise of surprise. Ellen's mother pushes her chair back. Grandpa is the coolest. Resting his hand on Nonie's shoulders, he examines Eva with frank curiosity. So does Ellen.

The dining room is even quieter than before. Eva stands over them, and Ellen can finally see her face.

So exaggerated! Like a mask, with her high cheekbones rouged and her lips widened like a clown's. And under the makeup are wrinkles. Thousands of wrinkles. Ellen looks into Eva's dark, sparkling eyes, her only feature that hasn't changed. Eva looks back. Looks back and recognizes her. Ellen is sure of it.

"I know you," Eva says suddenly, pointing at Ellen. "You're Eva."

Ellen's mother coughs. "No, she's *Ellen*. Fred's daughter. Your son Fred was my husband. You knew us once, but we haven't seen each other for years."

Eva's eyes glimmer. "Frederick's daughter!" she says, staring at Ellen.

Ellen feels her face burning.

Nonie gets up. "For heaven's sake, Dorothy, *let's go*."

Eva reaches out to Ellen. "Come here."

"No!" Nonie cries.

Grandpa takes Nonie's arm. "Okay, folks, time to go home."

The manager comes forward.

"Please help us," Nonie says shakily. "My husband's been ill, and this is very upsetting."

Ellen feels herself being propelled toward the door that the hostess is holding open for them. The manager stays between them and Eva.

"We're sorry, Mr. and Mrs. Kreider," the hostess whispers to Nonie and Grandpa. And then to Ellen's mother, "So sorry, Mrs. Dohrmann. She came in last week, too. We ask her not to, but—"

"It's not your fault," Ellen's mother says hastily.

Ellen can see that Eva is following.

"Come here!" Eva calls to Ellen.

"No." Ellen's mother stands in Eva's way. "I told you years ago. Ellen's not allowed to see you anymore. Please go home."

Then Ellen, urged outside by her mother, catches one last glimpse of Eva as the manager closes the door between them.

three

"Oh, oh! Thank the Lord." Nonie collapses in the back seat. "I thought for certain she was going to—I don't know what. Lock your door, Dorothy, Ellen. Keep your windows rolled up, *please*."

Dorothy locks her door and starts the motor.

Ellen, sitting rigidly in the front beside her mother, peers through the window until she can no longer see Eva standing under the canopy.

"And you, Frank—" Nonie, breathing heavily, locks the door on his side. "Are you sure you're all right?"

"Sure, sure," Grandpa says. "Don't worry about me."

14

"Well, I do. I worry about all of us." Nonie shivers. "I told you to have the party at our house tonight, didn't I, Dorothy?"

"Yes, but I couldn't predict this."

Grandpa leans forward. "Can't let her bother us. What's amazing is that it hasn't happened before. I've seen her on the street once in a while, but this business of coming right up and speaking to Ellen, well, that's something new. She hasn't been bothering you all along, has she, Ellen?"

"No."

"Well, I should hope not," Nonie says. "If she ever does again, you come right home, *please*."

Ellen doesn't answer.

Nonie shakes her head. "The way she helped herself to those tips! Brazen! And calling you *Eva*, of all things!"

As she drives up the bridge ramp, Ellen's mother glances at her. "You're sure she hasn't tried this sort of thing before, when you were alone?"

"This is the first time," Ellen says testily.

Her mother keeps looking at her.

"Ellen wouldn't do anything foolish," Nonie says. "She remembers the scare we had. What do you make of tonight, Dorothy? Do you think Eva knew who *we* were?"

Dorothy shifts uneasily behind the wheel as they rumble across the bridge. "I don't know."

Grandpa shakes his head. "Does she look like she

knows which end is up, wearing that fur thing in the middle of June? I say she doesn't know us from Adam. They say she's deteriorating fast."

Nonie raises her eyebrows. "Who says?"

"Why, the fellas at the bar, when she walked in there."

"You told them you're related, I bet. You think it makes a good story."

"Oh, everybody in town knows she's Doe's mother-in-law. That's not news. I just keep my mouth shut and listen. They were talking in the bar about the summer place her father had up on Tower Mountain. *Wunderlich.* It's being torn down, finally, to make way for condominiums."

Ellen turns around. "Torn down? It was such a neat place!"

"How do you remember?" her mother asks. Her face is tinged with blue under the bridge lights. "Oh, yes," she nods, "we drove by once or twice when we went up to Windsor Tower."

Ellen's voice is thin. "I visited *Wunderlich* with Eva."

Grandpa shakes his head. "You couldn't have, Ellie. Eva's father sold the place way back in the Depression. It sat there empty all these years, until just now a fellow's pulled it down to build apartments."

Nonie leans forward. "We never let you visit anywhere with her, Ellen."

16

Ellen, about to speak, closes her mouth. Her mother stirs behind the wheel.

Nonie lets out her breath. "I tell you, this whole evening has me so upset!"

"Got to take it in your stride, Mother," Grandpa says. "Ellen's no baby anymore. Are you, Ellie?"

"No!"

"Well, I worry," Nonie says. "I know Ellen's not a baby, but she's got a good heart, and she might go with Eva just to be polite."

Ellen sits up rigidly. "What if I did?"

"Oh, Ellen," Nonie says, "who *knows* what she's stealing these days or what else goes on in that East Windsor house?"

"Don't make stories, Mother," Grandpa interrupts. "She's crazy as a bedbug but harmless. Am I right, Doe?"

Dorothy drives off the ramp. "As far as I know."

"Think we have anything to worry about with Ellen?" Grandpa asks.

"I certainly hope not."

He's silent for a second. "Unless I pick Eva up and bring her over for a visit!"

"Oh, you're wicked, Frank. Just terrible! Isn't he, Dorothy?"

Grandpa taps Dorothy on the shoulder as she stops at a light. "Know the real reason your mother carries on so about Eva? Envy! She covets that big house in East Windsor and the three spiffy cars!"

"Oh, those cars," Nonie says, shaking her head. "They're older than Ellen, aren't they? They belonged to Eva's father. How is it they still run?"

Dorothy accelerates again. "The housekeeper's son used to take care of them for her. Maybe he still does."

Grandpa smiles. "Want me to make an offer for one of those buggies, Mother? Or for the fur tent, for your birthday?"

Nonie is quiet for a moment. "You know, I *did* envy her all the things she had in the old days, that's the truth. When we were girls. And look at her now! Oh, my, I wonder they don't arrest her!"

Grandpa shrugs. "The cops were always easy on her. I heard her father took care of them while he was alive. Who knows how it works, now that she lives off a trust fund. Have you heard anything lately from that lawyer, Doe?" Grandpa asks. "At the rate she's taking those tips, she should have a nice inheritance to leave to Ellen."

"Oh, Frank!" Nonie says.

"What lawyer?" Ellen asks.

Her mother turns onto Hill Avenue. "I got a letter some time ago from the law firm that handles her affairs. If Eva had an estate, Ellen, it would come to you as the only heir." She squints at the lights of an oncoming car. "I've always told myself, though, that it's not worth thinking about. We don't want anything from Eva. Besides, she'll be lucky if there's enough to keep her while she lives."

Nonie shakes her head. "How can a person who once had money *sink* like she has?"

Suddenly Ellen can't wait for the evening to be over. They turn left onto her grandparents' street. Let the good-nights be quick, Ellen thinks. As soon as the car pulls into the driveway, she pushes down the door handle. "I'll help you out," she says.

"Wait, dear." Nonie looks at Dorothy. "You'll stay, won't you? You and Ellen will sleep here tonight?"

"No, Mother," Dorothy says, to Ellen's relief. "We'll help you upstairs and go on home."

Ellen takes Grandpa's arm while her mother helps Nonie. They walk up the path between the neatly trimmed hedges.

Nonie reaches out to Ellen. "How about you staying over, birthday girl? You used to beg Mother to let you sleep here."

"I know," Ellen says, "but I have to go to the hospital tomorrow morning."

"Oh, my, I forgot you're working there again," Nonie says as she climbs the porch steps. "Seems like yesterday you almost *lived* with us summers. It all goes by so—" She stops suddenly at the sound of a motor. Headlights flash. A car slows to a crawl.

"Who's that, Frank?" Nonie asks. "Can you see who it is?"

Grandpa, holding onto Ellen, shrugs. "How would I know?"

"It's nobody, Mother," Dorothy says. "Go on in."

But Nonie waits until the car starts up again and disappears. Then she turns the key in the lock and motions them inside. "I know you think I'm foolish," she says. "To you she's harmless—a poor soul. I don't forget things so quickly, though. I still worry about Ellen."

four

Ellen's mother opens the door of the apartment and heads for the living room. "Come on in here and let's talk about this. I'm not sure I like your attitude."

Ellen closes the door harder than she means to. "What attitude?"

Her mother flicks on the lamp by the couch. "Oh, this attitude that nobody understands Eva, that nobody feels sorry for her but you." She takes off her glasses and rubs her eyes wearily. "We all feel sorry for her, Ellen. We always have! But Nonie and Grandpa and I know her, and we've learned that letting her go her own way is the only solution. We've gotten along fine these last seven years, haven't we, with that arrangement?"

Ellen starts down the hall to her room. "Forget it then. I don't want to talk about it."

"Ellen—"

"What?"

"Come here!" Her mother sinks into the sofa cushion, pats the one next to her. "Come on. Let's not end a nice birthday like this."

Ellen sits on the end of the couch, as far from her mother as possible. "You don't want to hear what I think," she says.

"That's what I mean about attitude!" her mother says, half annoyed, half puzzled. "You used to be so polite, so appreciative. Now you act as if we're on opposite sides in a debate. And as for me not wanting to hear what you think—you don't give me a chance. You don't *tell* me what you think!"

Ellen tries to concentrate, but her head feels heavy and her ears feel as if they're filled with water. She gazes around the room that she's known since they came back here when her father died— because Nonie and Grandpa expected them to. She focuses dimly on the flowered slipcovers, the coffee table, and the framed prints so like the wallpaper that they seem to disappear into it. Everything's *the same* in her life. Same surroundings, same volunteer job as last summer, same complaints about her attitude. She looks at her mother now, wishing she weren't put off by things her mother can't even help, like that hurt expression on her face, and that flowered print dress she's wearing, and the weight she's put on, even though she's a hospital dietician and ought to know better.

"Go ahead," her mother says, folding her arms. "Tell me what you think. I'm listening."

"All I said was I think it's stupid to sneak around town avoiding her, and I think it's terrible to treat her so badly."

"Badly? What do you mean?"

"Oh, Nonie practically faints, and Grandpa thinks she's funny, and you come off like a snob."

Her mother stares at her in silence for a second. "*I'm* a snob! That's funny. If you'd ever really known Eva Dohrmann, then you'd know what a snob is. Nonie could tell you better than I, how Eva and her father, when he was alive, thought they were the crown king and princess of this town. In that East Windsor mansion, with their works of art and fancy clothes and cars." Her mother closes her eyes. "Fortunately, Daddy had a completely different kind of life. He was raised by his father and went away to boarding school. If he'd grown up in Eva's house, I doubt that we would ever have gotten together."

Ellen glances at the photograph of her father on the mantel. "What did he do—just turn his back on her?"

"Not at all. He'd invite her to visit wherever we were stationed. He continued to visit her right up until he was sent to Vietnam. He had great compassion for her."

"So should we."

"We do. I feel I do!" her mother says. "It's just that no matter how much goodwill we'd show her, it wouldn't be enough. She's not an ordinary person, Ellen."

"I know that. I *know* her."

"You knew her when you were five, six, seven— a baby, almost."

"Until I was eight, and I wasn't a baby."

"Well, you saw only one side of her." Her mother sways forward. "I can see why you liked going there when you were little—to that big house, where they let you dress up in old clothes and play with everything, and where Eva and Alicia, the housekeeper, made such a fuss over you. 'We always have fresh strawberries for Ellen,' Alicia used to tell me when I brought you. 'Doesn't matter what season, fresh strawberries for Ellen!' "

"And little sandwiches in the living room or on the porch," Ellen says.

"That's what I mean. You had just one view of her—a fairy tale view. But I'd heard from Daddy how flighty she was as a mother. And I saw for myself how she got more and more peculiar over the years, so that when Daddy died, it was a big decision to come back here. It would have been a lot simpler in some ways, living away from Windsor."

Ellen sits up. "You didn't want to take me to see her, did you, when we came back?"

"No," her mother says wearily, "but I felt I had no choice. After all the losses she suffered, one after another—first her husband, then Daddy, then her father—you seemed to be the only person she cared about, and I told myself no harm would come of it. And then harm did come, of course."

"Can't you ever forget that?" Ellen says. "Seven years ago!"

"I guess I can't." Her mother shifts so that the couch creaks. "When you didn't come home from school that day—well, you'd have to be a mother yourself to imagine it."

"She picked me up at school, that's all!"

Ellen's mother touches her face as if it hurts. "It didn't occur to us that she was involved. We thought you'd been kidnapped."

"But you found me right away—"

"Not right away." Her mother's voice rises. "We spent two and a half hours in the police station before we found you at her house! And who knows how much longer it would have been, if that ring hadn't been reported stolen and the police hadn't suspected Eva?"

Ellen suddenly sits very still.

"I know you've never believed she took the ring," her mother says. "But she was seen in Main Avenue Jewelers the same afternoon. Everyone's aware that she takes things. Everyone's aware that she hoards jewelry. I'm as sure as I'm sitting here that she took it. It was worth quite a bit of money, too." She crosses her arms. "Anyway, I couldn't deal with that anymore—having her take you away like that, without permission, and seeing you involved in her wrongdoing. What kind of an influence would that have been on a child?"

Ellen remains silent.

"Don't you think we were right to break it off?" her mother asks.

Ellen's head is throbbing. "She's old now! Can't you forgive her?"

Her mother closes her eyes. "Forgive her, yes, but let you get mixed up with her again? No."

"She's all alone!"

"She wants it that way, Ellen," her mother says. "She's had a hard life, I admit. A mother who ran off when she was little. A father who kept her tied to him as long as he lived. A husband and son who died young. But other people have troubles, too, and they deal with them. They don't take things that don't belong to them, or carry off other people's children without asking. I've wrestled with this, Ellen, and I've made peace with myself about it. Eva doesn't need us. She's got a place to live, and a trust fund, and a woman to work for her, and a town full of agencies ready to help her if she asks. I did what I could for her once. But no more."

Ellen meets her eyes. "You're embarrassed by her, aren't you?"

"Oh, no," she says, shaking her head. "Maybe it

looks that way to you, but it isn't so. I stopped paying attention to the remarks about her a long time ago. The way I feel is, I'm as sorry for her as anybody, but I don't want to hear about her or see her, and I'm asking you to respect my wishes."

Ellen hesitates. "If I don't?"

The couch creaks again. "Well, then I'll be very disappointed. My main comfort in life since Daddy's death is that you're turning out so nicely—that I've never had to worry about you doing things that aren't sensible."

Ellen feels her face getting warm. "I'm tired of being sensible!"

Her mother pats her arm. "You're tired, period. It's been an upsetting evening for you." She smiles weakly. "Let's see if we can put this aside and have a nice, normal summer."

Ellen looks at her for a second. Then, sliding off the couch, she heads quickly for her room. "*You* have a nice, normal summer if you want to. I've had enough of them—they're boring!"

Ellen, in her nightgown, stands outside her mother's bedroom door. "Good night," she says.

The door opens.

Ellen raises her eyes. "Thanks for the present. It's really nice."

Her mother, in flowered pajamas, smiles. "You're welcome. I hoped you'd come to say good night." She pauses. "Can we try to have a good summer?"

"I'll try."

"Good. Better get some sleep now. Are you coming with me in the morning?"

Ellen nods.

"I ironed your uniform. It's in your closet."

"Thanks. Good night." She hesitates.

Her mother doesn't seem to notice. "Good night, and happy birthday!"

Ellen goes to her room and pulls down the spread that Nonie made for her by hand. She'd love to call Josie, but it's too late, so she snaps off the light, climbs into bed, and sits for a minute, staring at the spot where the streetlamp is reflected in her mirror. The eeriness used to scare her. Not anymore. She lies back, trying not to let the argument with her mother disturb her.

But it does. As usual. How can she be so annoyed at her mother, whose whole life is built around *her*? How can she be thinking mean things about that person across the hall, who, as far as Ellen knows, has slept alone in the big double bed for eleven years—putting her own happiness aside for Ellen's sake? If only her mother would quit being so protective and start living for herself, Ellen thinks. Or if she has to butt in, let her take a real interest. Let her ask about the good side of Eva—those quiet Saturday afternoons in the kitchen at East Windsor, making things and telling stories. Duets at the piano, and the parties on the porch, and the game she never told her mother about called "Going to

Wunderlich," where she and Eva packed a suitcase, drove up the mountain in one of Eva's cars, and roamed around the old summer place as if it still belonged to the family.

If her mother showed the slightest spark of interest in those things, she'd tell all, Ellen decides. She'd tell her about snooping around the cars and going with Josie on the bus to look at the house in East Windsor. She'd tell her how she almost spoke to Eva this afternoon in Zimmer's parking lot. What a relief it would be, to be able to tell after all this time.

A car goes by outside, and a light like the tail of a comet shoots across the mirror. She's willing to tell, but her mother doesn't want to hear. What her mother wants is a normal summer. Ellen shuts her eyes.

And if she goes against her mother's wishes? Before tonight that seemed impossible. But tonight Eva recognized her. Seven years later and both of them different, but Eva remembers her. What else does Eva remember?

Ellen opens her eyes and throws her legs over the side of the bed. Turning on the night light, she goes to her closet. For the first time in years, she lifts the fancy tin box down from the shelf and carries it back under the light. Then she opens it and takes out the square velvet box that's inside.

The lid snaps up and Ellen runs her finger over the white satin lining and the raised gold letters—

MAIN AVENUE JEWELERS. She looks at the purple stone in its old-fashioned setting that used to make her almost sick with nervousness when she'd touch it. Now she slips it on her finger next to the new aquamarine birthday ring.

Examining her hand under the lamp, Ellen still can't understand why the cops weren't more thorough that day. If they had as much as stared at her, she'd have confessed. And did Eva ever figure out that a small hand, feeling its way into the pocket of her cape, saved her from embarrassment—maybe even from arrest?

Ellen pulls off the ring with the purple stone, slips it into its two boxes, and puts it back on the shelf. If her mother had been more sympathetic tonight, Ellen would have shown her the ring. She's been dying to talk to somebody about it—this guilty souvenir that has helped her to keep on feeling connected to Eva. She's been on the brink of telling Josie about it several times, but Josie can't keep her mouth shut. That leaves only one person Ellen can think of to talk to. Maybe she'll go see Eva.

five

"Incredible." Josie crunches on an ice cube. "She *spoke* to you. Oh, God, why couldn't *I* have been there? Come on, tell me more. I want to know everything. Your mother *ordered* you to stay away from her?" She sticks her head out of the booth. "Another Coke, Trudy, when you get a chance."

The waitress, spatula in hand, scowls.

The smell of hamburger grease mingles in Ellen's nostrils with the faint medicinal odor that clings to her striped uniform. "It wasn't an order, it was an 'I'll-be-so-disappointed.'"

"Man, that Dorothy sure knows how to lay on the guilt trip." Josie adjusts her halter top. "What else? Nobody *did* anything when she ripped off the tips?"

"No."

"I love it!" Josie says, making a kissing sound. "What I love about her is that she does whatever she damn pleases. I mean, how many people in this world have the guts?"

"She's sad, Josie."

"She's *great*!" Josie's bangle bracelets clink as she leans her elbows on the table. "Did you ever think maybe she's pretending to be crazy?"

"You mean like Hamlet?"

"Never met the guy. Look." She prods Ellen. "Ben Bernhauser just came in. I think it's so excellent that he's wearing an earring. Who's that with him?"

Ellen turns around. "The other busboy at Zimmer's. They were there last night when it happened."

"No kidding. How did they react?"

"I don't know. They were in the kitchen."

Josie cranes her neck. "They just sat down in the front booth." She turns back to Ellen. "So. The important thing is she remembers you! When are we going to visit her?"

Ellen pauses. "What about my mother?"

Josie cups her hands to her mouth. "A Coke to go, please! Ellen," she says impatiently, "she remembers you. You're her only living blood relative. Besides, what your mother doesn't know won't hurt her."

"I hate being sneaky."

"Oh, you give me a pain sometimes. You're so straight!"

"No, I'm not."

"You are. Tell your mother then. I'll come with you for moral support."

"No."

"Well, I'm coming with you when you visit Eva, right?"

"If I go, I think it should be alone."

Josie meets a Coke halfway as it comes across the table. "Thanks, Trudy." She looks at Ellen. "You mean you don't want me to go with you? How come?"

"I do, but—"

"Hey."

Ellen raises her head. Ben Bernhauser is standing by the table. And the fat busboy, rubbing his glasses with his shirttail, is beside him.

"Ellen, Josie," Ben cracks his knuckles, "this is Buddha."

"Buddha?"

Buddha grins. "Barry Lightner. They call me Buddha because I'm wise. Right, Bernhauser?"

"Right. A real wise guy." Ben shifts his weight from one foot to the other. "He's Zimmer's nephew —working here for the summer. We get off early tonight, and we were wondering if you two want to go somewhere."

"Where?" Josie asks.

"Well." Ben rubs his neck, pulls his earring.

"Buddha's got a car and his uncle's got this pool—"

Josie looks at Ellen. "I could go after supper."

"Good. Suits optional," Buddha says.

Ellen and Josie exchange glances.

"Just kidding. My uncle's very against that, actually. We swim with our clothes on."

Josie slides out of the booth. "I've got to get back to work. I'll come if Ellen does. Call me, El."

Ben and Buddha follow Ellen down the aisle to the cash register.

"I have to ask my mother," she says.

"Hold it." Buddha grabs her arm. "No mothers invited."

Ben jabs him. "Shut *up*, man. You're making a lousy impression!"

"Where does your uncle live?" Ellen asks.

Buddha wipes his glasses on his shirt and puts them on again. "The *class* part of town. Country Club Road. Go on, ask your old lady. I'll behave myself, I promise."

six

"Hey, Ben! Ellen! Come on in—don't be so uptight!" A spurt of water arches from the pool, where Buddha makes a fountain of his hands. Ellen, sitting at the edge, feels a light spray hit her sandal.

"I swear, Ellen—it's so sensual to swim with your clothes on!" Josie, standing in the shallow end, hugs her dripping halter to her. "Much neater than skinny-dipping." She shivers. "Come on—jump in!"

"It's nice here," Ellen says, watching the lighted pool bottom, pock-marked and eerie as the surface of the moon. Ben, lying on his stomach a few yards away, skims his hand over the water and rescues a beetle.

In the deep end, Buddha's soaked shirt balloons out behind him like water wings. "You two gonna be sports, or do I have to throw you in?"

Ben stands up slowly. "I can't swim with clothes on." Unzipping, he drops his jeans.

"Ben!" Josie cries. "Oh, you've got a suit on!"

Ben swims the length of the pool underwater, while Buddha, with effort, pulls himself up the ladder. Water streams from this shirttails and from the frayed edges of his cutoffs as he shuffles toward Ellen.

"How come you're not having fun?" he asks, squinting without his glasses.

Ellen stands up. "I am. I'll come in in a minute. Where can I change?"

"Right here," Buddha makes a circle with his arms. "No, seriously, use any room in the house. My aunt and uncle went out. You sure you don't want any help? Getting wet, I mean. It's a cool experience."

"No thanks."

"Hold it." Buddha gropes on the deck for his glasses. "Before you put your suit on, how about riding along with me to get a couple of six-packs?" Adjusting the glasses on his nose, he digs the car keys from his pocket. "A little ride, okay?"

"I feel like swimming," Ellen says.

Buddha leans toward her confidentially. "Look, to be honest with you, Bernhauser asked me to leave him alone with your drippy friend there, and she's all for it. What do you say, shall we give them a break?"

Ellen turns toward the pool, where Ben is doing a racing stroke and Josie is floating, Ophelia-like, in shallow water. "Ben asked you that? And Josie agreed?"

"Give us fifteen minutes, they told me before. Fast workers." Buddha's eyebrows glisten with droplets of water. "Come on. We'll come back in *ten* and surprise 'em."

Ellen looks skeptically at him. "You're going like that?"

Pulling off his shirt, he picks up a towel and rubs his hairless chest and the fold of flesh at his middle. "Is that better?" He smiles.

"Wait a second." Ellen cups her hands to her mouth. "Josie! Josie, you want me to go with Buddha for beer?"

Josie, rising up, shakes like a sheepdog. "Beer? Yeah!" She sinks below the surface again.

Ellen glances at Ben swimming underwater.

Buddha nudges her. "Come on."

Ellen follows slowly. They cross the lawn in front of the sprawling ranch-style house. Even Buddha's feet are fat, she notices as he steps cautiously onto the pebbles of the driveway.

He squeezes into the old Volkswagen squareback and pushes open the door on her side. "Too bad this isn't next summer," he says. "By then I'll be driving my Porsche."

"You're getting a new car?" She leans back and reaches for a seatbelt that isn't there.

"A *Porsche*," he repeats. "For graduation."

"Didn't the real Buddha give up riches?"

"Ha! Hey, not this Buddha! *This* Buddha's religion is earning the bucks for car insurance." He turns the key. The motor hums. "Where's the nearest place for beer? How much can you and Josie handle—four cans apiece? More?"

"One will get warm before I finish it."

The VW, in reverse, whirrs and sputters over the pebbles with the sound of a popcorn machine.

"*One?*" Buddha switches gears. "I see I'm going to have to do some instructing this summer." He pumps his bare foot on the pedal and the VW lurches along past the golf course.

"Instructing who?"

"You," he says amiably. "In how to let loose, how to enjoy yourself more." Drifting through a stop sign, he sways close to her. "What year are you in, anyway—junior?"

"I'll be a sophomore."

"Oh, I'm a senior. One more year in the playpen. Not that I spend much time there. All my friends are out. I go around visiting colleges a lot."

Ellen looks out the window at the houses, smaller and closer together now that they're approaching the heart of Windsor. "Which colleges have you visited?" she asks distractedly.

"Hell, all the best party schools. You wouldn't

believe the weekends I had last year." Honking, he passes a motorcycle. "At this one school up in Maine, we played Quarters straight through from Friday till Sunday. You know Quarters? Great drinking game. I'll teach you when we get back to my uncle's. Where the hell's this store I thought was here?"

He makes a left. "Man, I used to think where *I* come from was beat. At least my town's only an hour from New York City. What was I saying before? Oh, yeah, wild weekends. At this one frat party, at three in the morning we all played Post Office."

"Wasn't that kind of junior high school?"

"Not this kind of Post Office. I mean the kind where you pull up a mailbox—one of those red and blue jobs, cement post and all. It's a federal offense, you know. Anyway, we took this uprooted mailbox back to the frat house in a van and hid it in a closet." Buddha's eyes are magnified behind his glasses. "The F.B.I. came around a week later, I heard, but I was home free by then. Where the hell is that store?" His bare foot slides off the gas pedal. "There it is! Budweiser!"

"The store's closed."

Buddha thumps one hand on the wheel. "What's *with* this town, anyway? Is anything open after five P.M.?"

"Not much. We may as well go back."

"I don't give up that easy." Grinding gears, he

makes a U-turn. "I'll go to the Square if I have to. To the restaurant. The bartender'll slip me some. You know," he says as he heads downtown, "this isn't funny anymore. I'm afraid I'll go bananas staying here all summer. My first night here—get this!—my uncle tells Bernhauser to show me Windsor. Know what we did? Sat in the Square sharing a Dr Pepper and counting lightning bugs." Buddha jams on the brake at the light. "Second night I went straight home by myself. Fell asleep watching an old Ronald Reagan movie."

The VW jolts forward again. "Last night—shot down again! When we got off work we saw this character in front of the restaurant. This mental old lady dressed in *fur*. I had this great idea of—well, never mind. Bernhauser spoiled all my fun. Dragged me over to his house. Know the lady I'm talking about?"

"Yes," she says evenly. "I know who you mean." Up ahead, the clock of the Franklin Building glows.

Buddha sails through a yellow light. "What's her story? Did living in this town drive her nuts?"

"Maybe."

"I can dig that." He chuckles. "Look at your friends: Josie—sixteen, and dippy already! And Bernhauser—"

Ellen, looking down the dark side street, fixes her eyes on an unexpected sight there. She keeps glancing back at it as Buddha drives into the Square.

40

"What's with Bernhauser, anyway?" Buddha asks.

"What do you mean?"

Pulling into a parking space, Buddha shuts off the motor. "Is he—I mean, with that earring and all—is he a faggot?"

"If he were," she says, "why would he ask you to leave him alone with Josie?"

Light reflects off Buddha's glasses. He smiles. "He didn't ask me. Neither did she. I made that up."

Ellen turns away from him.

"Hey, you aren't mad, are you?" He lays his hand on her shoulder.

Shaking free, Ellen stares at the line of parked cars and the sidewalk ahead, and at the red and white canopy of Zimmer's. "How about getting the beer? I can't stay too much longer."

"Come with me. Come on."

"No. Not in the bar."

"We'll go in the back way."

"No. I'll wait here. Hurry up."

Buddha, opening the door, squeezes out from behind the wheel. "Be right back."

As soon as he has disappeared inside the restaurant, Ellen opens the car door.

The Square is deserted except for a couple on their way into Zimmer's. Ellen gets out. After a quick look behind her, she retraces the route she and Buddha have just traveled. At Plummer's Department Store she turns down the side street.

Just as before, there's a car parked in front of the one lighted storefront. The determination she felt a few minutes ago is fading a little, but she forces herself to go on. Who knows how long she may have to wait for another chance like this? A chance to walk directly up to the maroon car where Eva is sitting with the door slightly open, as if she's expecting her.

seven

Eva has no idea she's being watched. Ellen, standing with one hand on the dented rear fender, has a pretty good view because of the light coming from Max's Fur Emporium. The screws holding Eva's license plate are loose, she notices, and the plate is outdated.

Eva, behind the wheel, seems to be talking to herself. She moves jerkily so that her hat falls off, and Ellen sees her bend over to pick it up.

Ellen opens the car door all the way. "Here, I'll get it for you," she says. She gropes for the hat and at the same time pushes aside some junk to make space for herself on the front seat. "You know me, don't you?" she asks.

Eva squints at her and sets the hat back on her

head. Ellen, breathing in the musty odor of the car's interior, absorbs as many details as she can in the dim light. The space above the dashboard is crammed with small objects: a hand mirror, books of matches, a hammer. Under Ellen's feet are boxes that rattle when she bumps them. Between Eva and herself on the front seat is the guitar and a lamp shade. The back seat is packed almost to the ceiling with newspapers. The clock in the dashboard says 9:05. Good! Ellen thinks. She can still make it home by ten, as her mother asked her to.

Finally. *Finally*, Ellen thinks, shaky but elated as she peers over the guitar. Eva's made-up cheeks and lips are deep purple in the fluorescent light. Her gloved hands, heavy with rings, clutch the steering wheel. Is she angry, or is it just the slant of her penciled eyebrows? Ellen swallows. "I can't stay long," she begins hesitantly. "I had to speak to you, though. Is it all right if I close the door?"

Eva makes no protest.

Ellen slams it and the smell inside is overpowering. "I just want to know if you're all right," she says breathlessly. "That's the main thing. I've wanted to see you for a long time, but my mother thought I shouldn't. She's still upset about . . . that day." Ellen pauses. "I shouldn't blame *her*, really. Let's just say I put off seeing you until now." She glances at Eva. Is it possible she's hard of hearing?

Ellen speaks louder. "You probably never realized it, but I've kept track of you all this time. I watch for you when I'm downtown. I even came by your house a few times." She smiles, but Eva is still stonefaced.

Ellen goes on impulsively. "The reason I'm here now—well, it's partly chance, but I told myself I *would*—is that last night in Zimmer's I was sure you remembered me. You said, 'I know you,' and I thought there was something between us. Is there?" she asks faintly, watching Eva in the bluish light. "Can you hear me at all?"

Eva's eyes are riveted on her, but there is so little sign of understanding that Ellen considers leaving as abruptly as she came. She tries again. "Please say something. Please say you remember me. Fred's daughter—?"

There is a slight movement of Eva's hands on the steering wheel.

"I don't blame you for being confused," Ellen blurts out. "I must look pretty different after seven years. I thought maybe you recognized me because of my eyes. They're supposed to be like my father's and yours. And my Dohrmann shape." She pats her hips. "My mother and Nonie are big-boned, you know, and sort of round. I'm a skinny Dohrmann." Ellen looks at the loose, dark-colored dress under Eva's fur cape. "You've lost weight, haven't you? I noticed last night."

Eva glances down at herself, the first sign she has understood.

"You're not sick, are you?" Ellen asks quickly.

"Because, if there's something wrong, I work at Windsor General, as a candystriper, a volunteer. I could take you there. I work weekdays. So does my mother. She's a dietician, but she knows lots of doctors. Is something the matter?"

Eva shakes her head.

"Good." Ellen leans back against the plush seat. She can feel lumpy objects poking her on both sides. "There's so much I want to tell you," she goes on, now that Eva seems to be listening. "I've thought about you so much—about you and the house and the Saturdays I spent there. How is the house?"

Eva doesn't answer.

Keep trying. She spoke last night. She can speak. "Do you still have the clothes you used to let me try on?" Ellen asks. "And those things in the trunk—the beaded bags and the fans? And the stuffed deer in the living room, that I used to climb up on? And the dollhouse—in the summer kitchen, where there was that swinging door for the dog! Toby! How is—?"

"No more," Eva says curtly.

"He got lost, or—? Oh well, sure. He must have been an old dog even then." Ellen pauses. Eva's voice sounds so hoarse. "Is Alicia still with you?" Ellen asks.

Eva's head quivers, a habit Ellen remembers. "When I call her."

"She doesn't live in anymore? It must be hard

46

for you to keep up the whole house. How *is* the house? My mother doesn't think I remember much, but I do. *Everything*. How about that couch with the heart-shaped back? And that painting of you, where you said we looked alike?"

Eva's lips twitch, the hint of a smile.

"Remember the games we used to play?" Ellen goes on excitedly. "Tic-tac-toe and Parcheesi and 'Going to *Wunderlich*'? And how we used to make roses out of tissue paper and put perfume on them? And the piano! Remember playing 'Flow Gently Sweet Afton' on that huge piano in the music room?"

"Shhh!" Eva raises a ringed finger to her lips.

"What?"

"He mustn't know!" she whispers.

"About playing the piano? Who mustn't know?"

"Shhh! No more!"

Ellen looks at her with curiosity. Is it an old game she's forgotten? She shifts so that the springs of the seat squeak. "I hope you'll let me come see the house soon," she says, changing the subject. "If there's anything to be done, I could help."

Eva's necklaces jangle as she sways at the wheel. Then, to Ellen's surprise, she drops one hand and turns the key in the ignition. The motor sputters, then hums.

Ellen lurches forward. "What are you doing?"

"Going home," Eva says.

"To your house?" Ellen pauses. "Oh, I didn't

mean *tonight*. I'd like to, but it's late and I told my mother I'd be home at ten. She thinks I'm with—"

Eva's sneaker presses down on the accelerator. The motor races. "Come," she says.

Ellen touches the cape. "Grandma Eva," she says, using the name for the first time in years, "I will come, I swear. But not now. Tomorrow, after work. Okay? You can show me around the house and we'll talk some more. I'll come at about four." She looks at the dashboard, where the clock still says 9:05. "Oh, no, your clock's stopped!" Ellen opens the door. "I must be late already."

"*Come*," Eva urges.

"I can't now, really. But don't worry—I'll be there at four tomorrow. You know me now, don't you? You believe me?"

"Frederick's daughter," Eva murmurs.

"That's right!" Ellen stands on the curb. "Be careful now, okay? I'll see you tomorrow. Good night!"

Ellen isn't sure what to expect as she backs away from the maroon car, but she sees it buck forward and in another minute Eva has gone down the street and turned toward East Windsor.

eight

*S*he did it. She spoke to Eva! Ellen sits down on the bench by the bus stop. It's late. The Square looks ghostly. She should call her mother right away. She can't, though. She can't do anything but sit here, going over it all again. *Eva remembers her, wants to see her tomorrow.* Ellen is so involved in her thoughts that at the first sound of footsteps behind her, she's sure Eva has come back. It isn't until she jumps up that she sees it's not Eva at all, but Ben Bernhauser.

"Hey. What happened? Where've you been, for Pete's sake?" Ben's thumbs are stuck in the waist of his beltless jeans. His hair is messed up—still wet, probably, though Ellen can't see very clearly.

She comes toward him. "I got out of Buddha's

49

car because I . . . saw someone. I'm sorry if—" She breaks off. "Where is Buddha?" she asks giddily. "Where's Josie? What are you doing here?"

"Josie and Buddha are driving around looking for you," Ben says. "They dropped me off here to check the Square." Ben rises up on the toes of his sneakers. "So. What's the story? Who'd you run into, Robert Redford?"

"My grandmother," she says quickly. "Eva."

"Oh. Yeah. Well." He shifts his weight. "Do you talk to her often?"

"No. This is the first time in seven years."

"No kidding. I didn't realize." He shrugs. "Just like that? Out of the blue?"

"No. I've been thinking about it." She glances at the clock. "I'm glad you found me. Is Buddha coming back for you?"

"I'm not counting on it." Ben pats down his tousled hair with both hands. "He wasn't in too good a mood, actually. The bartender wouldn't give him anything, you took off on him, and then Josie accused him of attacking you. He's kind of down on Windsor at this point. Hell, we don't even have a Porsche dealership." Ben slaps his hands together. "Look, the last bus left already, and my Porsche is in for servicing—want to walk? I'll protect you from the Windsor Werewolf."

"It's far for you—"

"What the heck. I can sleep late. I don't have to be at work until late in the afternoon." They cross the street near Zimmer's. "Can't seem to stay away from this place, can we?"

"No." She looks up at him. "You heard what Eva did last night, didn't you?"

"Yeah."

"You didn't tell him she's my grandmother."

"Hell no. Why should I?"

Ellen looks up at him. The little gold star in his ear looks good, actually. They wait at the corner for a car to go by.

"Yeah," Ben says, "she's been in once or twice since I started working. I keep my eyes open, but I never say anything to anybody about her."

They begin the long trek up West Main Avenue. Ben's long skinny shadow dwarfs Ellen's as they pass under the streetlamp. Up ahead, the light on the marquee of the Rialto Theater goes out.

"What does she do when she comes in?" Ellen asks.

"Takes tips. Takes leftover rolls and stuff. Never orders anything or talks to anybody. Never drinks. I thought all these years maybe she's a wino, but that's not her problem, is it?"

"No. Does anybody try to talk to her?"

Ben sticks his hands in his pockets. "The manager says nothing. I think he's afraid of her. The waitresses buzz to each other. Some of the guys in the bar bait her, but she's very cool. No reaction."

Ellen gazes ahead at the lights on the bridge.

"How would you act if she were your grand-mother?"

"Ho. Well. Act?" Ben plucks at his T-shirt. "The way you do, I guess. You've always seemed pretty together about her."

Ellen shakes her head. "I'm a fake. I'm not together at all."

"Hey, who *is*? What I like is that you don't pretend she's a stranger. And you don't go along with the mocking. You just take her like she is. Man," he says, clapping his hand to his thigh. "I'm just now getting this incredible picture of you hopping out of Buddha's car and talking to her for the first time in seven years! What did you say to each other?"

Ellen slows her pace as they head toward the walkway of the bridge. "I did most of the talking. I asked her how she is. I told her I've wanted to see her for a long time—"

"How come you haven't?"

"My mother and my grandparents don't think I should."

Ben slows to keep even with her. "Afraid of what the neighbors'll say?"

"Oh, it's more that they think she'll be a *bad influence* on me."

"Sounds familiar. I get that kind of stuff all the time. So what did your grandmother say to you?" he asks.

Ellen looks over the bridge railing. "She wanted me to go home with her. Tonight."

"No kidding. You said no?"

"I told her tomorrow."

"I was there once," Ben says. "Inside the house, I mean."

"When?"

Ben runs his fingers along the guard rail of the bridge. "Oh, I was ten, maybe—all by myself, walking past her place. I live just a couple of blocks from her, you know. She was standing in the driveway. So she sees me and says, 'Come here, young man.' In this very *rich* voice. Like a queen, you know? She looked like one, too." Ben laughs. "I felt like running for the hills. You must have heard those stories. Kids used to say there was a body in the house. You heard that, am I right?"

"Yes. Go on. You went over to her?"

"Yeah, yeah. I'm scared, but I go. She's standing by one of her cars, and she says, 'Carry this into the house, young man. I'll pay you.' It was this portable phonograph, the kind you wind by hand. So I pick it up. She leads me, and all the time I'm thinking, *So long, Benjamin, nice knowin' ya!*"

"You're here to tell about it."

"Yeah. So she takes me through the living room —well, you've seen it. I've heard she doesn't take care of it now. But then it was like in a movie— *Citizen Kane*. With that huge fireplace and statues and stuff. Next she takes me up the stairs to this door that was locked.

"The music room."

"Who knows? 'Put it down,' she tells me. 'No one enters this room.' That's where the body is, I think to myself. Man, did I drop that record player! I zoom down the stairs, and she's hot on my tail, calling 'Wait, young man!' Well, I wait, out of fear, or whatever, until she catches up with me and I realize she just wants to pay me.

" 'This is for you,' she says. I expect Monopoly money or a quarter or something, but it was a ten-dollar bill." He smiles. "So from then on, I always defend her."

Ellen laughs. At the end of the bridge is Palmer Park. Fireflies are glowing. The smell of freshly cut grass drifts toward her. "I remember good things about her, too," Ellen says. "I thought I was the only one."

"No. She must've been some great lady once. What's her story? Husband leave her, or what?"

"I don't know much about him," Ellen says. "She lived with her father mostly. When he died, she got much worse, my mother says."

"Yeah? How old is she now?"

"Seventy."

"She stays all alone in that big place?"

"Yes, she used to have a live-in housekeeper, but now she's alone, as far as I know."

Ben cracks his knuckles. "Think she'd be better off somewhere else?"

"Away from her house? No! I've been thinking, there're a lot of things I can do for her, now that I—"

"Maybe," Ben says, cutting her off. "Sounds like that could be a pretty heavy trip, though—having her depend on you." He leads the way up Hill Avenue. "Did anybody ever suggest putting her in a hospital?"

Ellen stops. "You mean committing her to Crocker State? Oh, *please*. All I've ever heard makes me sick just thinking about that place. Remember in grade school how the kids used to do these gross imitations and say, 'I'm off my rocker, call up Crocker!' "

Ben, in the shadows, waits for her. "There must be a decent hospital somewhere. My grandfather's in this pretty good nursing home. He had no choice. Both of his legs had to be amputated, and my grandmother couldn't lift him. We thought it was going to be hell, but he actually likes the place. He hangs out with these other old guys, telling them bits like, 'I took my surgeon to court, but I lost the case. The judge said I didn't have a leg to stand on!' "

Ellen, smiling, coming close to Ben, has a sudden urge to ask him why he pierced his ear. Josie would ask. Must be nice to do whatever you feel like doing. "Ben," she says instead, "I need some advice. My mother asked me to stay away from Eva. Should I tell her what happened tonight or not?"

Ben, stumbling over a crack in the sidewalk, catches himself. "Watch it." He reaches out to support her. "I'd say, do what makes you feel right. I'm a big help, aren't I?"

"You were," Ellen says. "The Windsor Werewolf didn't get me." She can see the light now, the one her mother leaves on until Ellen gets home. "Thanks a lot, really. I think what I'll do is once I've been there, then I'll tell my mother. After I've proved that it's no big deal."

They walk up the path. Ben lays his hand on her arm. "You're pretty wound up, aren't you?"

"Yeah. I guess so. I've thought about Eva for so long."

"And now she's back in your life. How do you feel?"

"Relieved," Ellen says as they climb the porch steps. "I can finally *do* something."

"I hope everything works out." Ben looks up. "This is a two-family, isn't it? You live upstairs?"

She nods.

He sways forward for a moment as if he's going to touch her again, but instead he puts his hands behind his back and leans on the railing. "What a weird night." He slaps the railing with his palm. "Look, if there's anything I can do—"

"Do you think you could call Josie and tell her

I'm okay? Tell her I can't meet her at Giese's tomorrow after work. Don't mention where I'm going. I'll tell her myself, afterward."

"How about Buddha? What should I tell him?"

"That I ran off with Robert Redford." She can see Ben's lean face and the tiny gold star in his ear as he turns and lifts one leg over the porch railing. Now that he has his back to her, Ellen can also see a bit of red, like a handkerchief, sticking out of his pocket.

Ben jumps to the ground. "Let me know what happens," he calls, jogging down the path.

"I will. Thanks. Where will you be?"

"Home tomorrow until four."

Her eyes shift to the ground beneath the railing. She goes down the steps and leans over. "Ben! Ben, you dropped your bathing suit!"

No answer.

She considers following him, but instead she folds the damp suit neatly and puts it in her bag. Then she unlocks the door and goes up the stairs. If she's lucky, her mother will be in bed already and too tired to ask her why she's so late.

nine

Ellen pushes the stainless-steel cart past the nurses' station.

"Just those few rooms on Two West, Ellen," Mrs. Fields tells her. "Then you can leave. I bet you're going to jump right in a swimming pool, aren't you? Nice warm afternoon like this!"

"Sounds great," Ellen says.

Mrs. Fields raises her plump arms to adjust her nurse's cap. "You're waiting for Mom, is that it? She'll drive you home?"

"No, not today." Ellen makes her way along the West Wing. No swimming this afternoon. No going home, either.

A doctor passes by without greeting her, and the name of another doctor is called urgently over the

P.A. Ellen stops to make sure there's enough ice in her container. Then she wheels the cart into Mr. Sloan and Mr. Gunderson's room.

"Oh boy, oh boy, here she comes!"

"A pretty girl? Is that you, Ellen?"

"Why, sure it's Ellen. Come here, Ellen. How about putting a little extra something in that ginger ale! Couldn't you do that for an old friend of your Grandpa Kreider?"

"Ho, is *that* who this pretty little girl is? Ellen— what's her last name?"

"Dohrmann! Don't you know, *Dohrmann?*"

Ellen hands them their ginger ale in silence. "See you Monday," she says.

"Going so soon? What kind of service is that?"

"Shush! Don't pay any attention to him, Ellen. You go on to the younger fellas now. Say hello to Grandpa, you hear me?"

"I will."

In the next room Mrs. Pfaff is dabbing her damp forehead with a balled-up tissue. "Would you like something to drink, Mrs. Pfaff?" Ellen asks. "Orange juice, apple, cranberry, ginger ale?"

"Oh my, yes. Cranberry please. Such a good girl!"

Ellen pours.

"How old are you, dear?"

"Fifteen."

"Isn't that wonderful! Wait a minute, I want to show you something. Open that drawer, dear, and hand me those cards." Riffling through a packet of mail, she holds up a photograph. "My granddaughter is fifteen! Isn't that something?"

Ellen looks at the worn snapshot of a girl in a ski jacket. "She looks nice," Ellen says.

"You're right, dear, she is. Breaks my heart I don't see her." She pauses. "You live here in Windsor? You come in every day?"

"Weekdays."

"Well, I surely wish you could stay awhile. Can you stay?"

"I . . . I have to take the cart back to the kitchen. I'm about to go off now." Ellen starts to leave.

Mrs. Pfaff sinks back on her pillow and dabs her forehead again. "Another time, then. I'll be here all next week."

"I'll see you then," Ellen says. "Good-bye."

"*Dr. Ferrara to the sixth floor. Dr. Ferrara to the sixth floor.*"

What's it like? Ellen wonders, as she hears the urgent call. Sixth-floor psychiatric ward. What do they do up there? She pushes her cart over the shiny tile floor toward the nurses' station.

"Your girl friend just phoned you," Mrs. Fields calls to her. "Josie. She says she's coming over here to meet you and don't you leave without her." She smiles. "You can go along now. I'll take your cart back."

"Thanks a lot. Have a nice weekend." Ellen's head feels fuzzy as she signs out and changes into her own clothes. What should she do about Josie? In the hall Ellen presses the button for the elevator, and she looks around cautiously when the doors open on the ground floor. Instead of her usual way, Ellen goes out the exit near the Emergency Room. Taking a short cut through the hospital rose garden, she heads for the bus stop. The bus to East Windsor comes within a few minutes, and Ellen gets on it, convinced that the best way to visit Eva is by herself.

Ellen gets off the bus. It's been so long since she was here that she's forgotten how big the houses are along the boulevard. On the corner, behind a hedge, is Johnson's mansion, with a sports car in the driveway. Then comes Riegels'. Her mother's words come back to Ellen as she passes Riegels' English garden. *If Eva left an estate, Ellen, it would come to you.* Maybe Eva's got a lot of money hidden somewhere. Or maybe the house itself will be left to her, Ellen thinks. Would she live in it? Sure—and give big parties, and invite friends to stay over, and hand it down to her children, if she has any.

The fantasy is cut short, though, by her first sight of the place. She stops on the sidewalk, in front of the crumbling wall. The grass is waist-high, clogged with thistles and leaves. And the rambling, Spanish-style white stucco house is a dingy gray now. Broken roof tiles are heaped in a pile in front of the main entrance. And the entrance looks boarded up. She comes through the gateposts. Several windows are cracked. A garage door lies flat on the ground. The last time she saw the place it was run-down, but not like this.

The knot in her stomach grows tighter as she walks along the driveway, where only two cars are parked. Eva's not here. She's forgotten about their appointment.

Unless one car is out for repairs. Ellen pauses again, trying to see the house for a minute as it was when she was little, with its wicker furniture on the porches and boxwood trees outlining the garden.

Now the porches are bare and the boxwoods are brown and leafless. Boards crisscross the doorway as if nobody lives here. Should she go away and come back another time? Not until she's certain Eva isn't here.

The grass whips at her bare legs as she crosses the yard and climbs the steps of the side porch. This was the entrance they used most, she remembers. The urns are still here, but without any flowers in them. The stone lions she loved to sit on are greenish and pockmarked, but the cement bench is exactly the same to her touch, and the French doors are standing partly open as they always did on warm afternoons.

Ellen knocks, but no one comes. "Grandma Eva?" she calls.

The only sound is the hum of insects in the tall grass. She peers through the space between the

French doors, into the darkness of the living room, where most of the drapes are pulled. Should she go in and wait? After all, it's her own grandmother's house. Maybe *her* house someday. Ellen pulls the doors open and enters the living room.

There she stands, breathing shallowly, unable to believe what she sees. She loved this room once— loved the walk-in fireplace, the elegant furnishings. Now the Oriental rugs barely show under the remnants of carpet that Eva must have brought home from a dump. Up and down the huge room, boxes and newspapers are stacked wall-to-wall, with just one narrow path from the doors to the staircase. In one corner is the skeleton of a Christmas tree. By the staircase, a large metal wardrobe. The living room is a warehouse for Eva's junk. How can she live here?

Ellen would like to call out again, but she's not sure of her voice. Sitting on a straight-backed chair, she stares at the dust motes dancing in the shafts of sunlight where a drapery has come down. The longer she looks, the more painful it is to see what's become of the things she remembers. The heart-shaped couch is blocking the main entrance, the deer's antlers are hung with hats, the top of the desk is cluttered with debris.

Is it possible that Eva is here somewhere, in another room? Ellen inches forward, prodding cartons with her foot, touching dusty lamps. What would her mother say if she saw her now? She bumps the desk, and the lid drops open. Ellen moves back as an avalanche of mail slides to the floor. Envelopes of all sizes and types spill at her feet. She picks up one, then another, and turns them over in her hands. Some have postmarks that go back a year or more. Most of them are sealed, but a few have been opened. Ellen looks at the return addresses: one that has to do with taxes; one from the Windsor Sanitation Department; and another from a Philadelphia company called Burgess, Redington and Hintz. Bristling with curiosity, she is about to take one of the letters out of its envelope when she hears a sound behind her. She turns, surprised to see Eva, bag over her arm, standing by the French doors.

ten

"Hi." Ellen, her voice catching, lets the envelope drop. "Hi. I came, like I said I would."

Eva makes her way slowly over to the desk. Under the fur cape Ellen sees the same dark dress Eva wore the night before. Eva's hat this time is a man's gray felt with a feather stuck in a wide band.

Unsure of what to do with her hands, Ellen clamps them together as she's seen Ben do. "I . . . at first I was going to go away when you weren't here," she says. "Then I decided to come in and wait. I hope you don't mind. Some letters fell on the floor. Sorry if I—"

Eva reaches the desk and they stand eye to eye. She looks at Ellen as if she's used to seeing her here.

"You didn't forget I was coming, did you?" Ellen asks. "Did you have to go out?"

"Yes, yes."

Ellen forces a smile. Close up and in daylight, Eva's face shocks her. The features are sharp. Unlike Nonie, whose extra pounds fill her out, Eva is gaunt. Skin hangs loosely at her neck. Her hair is hidden under the hat, and the rouge caked over wrinkles makes her face look like a dry riverbed. Ellen tries to ignore the odor, but she can't. Eva needs a bath.

"It's a nice day," she says awkwardly. "Did you go out for a ride?"

For an answer, Eva opens her bag and, as Ellen watches, takes out a chipped vase that she places on top of the cluttered desk.

"Nice," Ellen says hesitantly.

Next Eva takes a few old postcards out of her bag and stuffs them into a pigeonhole of the desk.

"Don't you think some of that mail should be taken care of?" Ellen asks as gently as she can.

Eva snaps the lid shut. "Alicia does that."

"Oh. Are you sure she still comes? I mean, can we call her?"

"No, no, not now." Eva, taking a plastic fork from her bag, motions toward the dining room.

Ellen goes first between the rows of cartons and piles of newspapers. "Wouldn't it be better to move these things? You'd have much more room to get around."

66

"No, no, I'm not moving."

Ellen trips over a plank of wood. "Oh, you wouldn't have to do it yourself. We could get somebody."

"No strangers!"

Ellen looks at her in surprise. "I could move the things."

"No. I need them here," Eva says.

Ellen arrives at the double doors between the living and dining rooms. She can hear Eva shuffling behind her. Ellen turns the knob, but the door doesn't open.

"Here, here." Eva steps in front of her and pushes. Ellen helps her, so that the door finally opens wide enough for the two of them to squeeze into the dining room.

"Can't we put this somewhere else?" Ellen asks, shoving the heavy wooden trunk that has been blocking their way.

"No, no. It goes back when we finish in here."

Ellen takes her hands off the trunk. "Why? It's not safe, Grandma Eva." She stares at the dining room chairs that form a barricade at the set of French doors on this side of the house. "All these closed-off doorways are dangerous," Ellen says. "What if you have to get out in a hurry?"

"I keep *them* out," Eva says curtly.

"Keep *who* out?" Ellen feels the knot in her stomach again.

"The strange men who want my things," Eva

says, laying the plastic fork from her bag at the head of the table.

Ellen notices several plastic place settings spaced at intervals along the dining room table. "Is this where you eat?" she asks weakly.

"Well, of course, when he's here."

Opening her mouth, Ellen decides not to say what she intended. She peers through the semi-darkness at the heavy drapes pulled across all the windows. "Wouldn't you like to let some light in?" she asks. "How about turning this on?" Ellen flicks the switch to the chandelier, but it doesn't light up. She looks at Eva, puzzled, then tries the switch again. "Are you sure you have electricity?" she asks. "Do the lights work in the kitchen?" Giving the door a push, Ellen goes into the kitchen, with Eva trailing behind her.

Daylight filters through the dirty window over the sink. The door to the outside is padlocked, but otherwise the room is recognizable. There's the old sink on legs, where Ellen used to crouch with her ear pressed against the gurgling pipe. And the metal table, where she and Eva used to make paper roses and write their initials in fancy letters on long sheets of paper. And there's the other locked door that leads out to the summer kitchen where the dollhouse was, and where Toby the dog used to come in and out through a special little opening made just for him. The layout of the kitchen is still the same, but a film of dirt covers everything—

countertops, table, and stove. The little mosaic tiles on the floor, once white, are dark gray now.

"The kitchen hasn't been used," Ellen says. "Do you ever make meals for yourself?"

"No fuss," Eva says with a shrug. "Oh, I can be a hostess he isn't ashamed of, if that's what you're worried about. Don't listen to Alicia!"

Ellen's stomach clenches tighter. "Grandma Eva, do you have food for tonight?"

"I've got something in here," she says, patting her bag.

"What? Rolls from Zimmer's?"

Eva, feeling around with one gloved hand, holds up a roll triumphantly.

Ellen feels tears spring to her eyes. "Do you need money, Grandma Eva? My mother says you have a trust fund, but if it's not enough, I can give you some. I have money in the bank—"

"That's Alicia's concern," Eva says impatiently.

"Then why don't you call her!" Ellen struggles to bring her voice under control. "Is there electricity in here?" She flips the switch, but the kitchen lights don't go on, either.

Moving to the range next, Ellen turns on the jet, blows on the burner, puts her nose close to it. "No gas," she murmurs aloud. She hurries to the sink and turns on the faucets with both hands. No water comes out. Then she throws open the doors of the refrigerator. It's empty. Only the odor remains, and the pattern of gray mold on the door and the walls. Ellen covers her face with her hands now, partly to block out the sight and the smell, and partly to hide the tears that are rolling down her cheeks. The house she once loved is a wreck, yes, but houses can be repaired. What do you do when a *person* you loved is—

Ellen can't stop herself. She lets go of the tears, sobbing softly. Eva, watching her, makes no move, as Ellen stands there in the grimy kitchen and thinks of a time when she would have been hugged by Eva and taken to see the dollhouse to get her mind off whatever was bothering her. Now Eva is picking idly at her rings with her free hand, and the dollhouse may or may not still be back there, behind the padlocked door. "I—I guess I'll go now," Ellen whispers.

Eva snaps out of her trance. "No, no. Come."

Ellen looks at her uncertainly. "Where?"

Eva points upward. "Don't tell. He doesn't permit it, you know. Come."

Ellen, wary but curious, follows Eva through the dining room, past the trunk, and into the junk-filled living room. To the right of the staircase Ellen sees a door that leads, through a storage room, to the summer kitchen. Bumping against the metal wardrobe at the bottom of the stairs, she looks up at the oil portrait hanging over it. The painting is of Eva at age twelve or so, prim and neat in a white dress. *That's* the Eva Ellen would give anything to have known. Climbing the steps behind her grandmoth-

70

er as she used to do years ago, Ellen has forgotten for the moment her feelings of frustration. "Where are we going?" she asks playfully.

Eva presses her finger to her lips again. At the top of the steps she reaches under her cape for one of the chains and comes up with a key, which she slips into the lock of the first door on the left.

"The music room," Ellen says. She thinks of Ben.

"Shhh!" Eva warns sharply as she opens the door.

They step into the room.

And, to Ellen's amazement, the music room is just as she remembers it. Light, pouring through the shutters, makes the grand piano gleam. The piano and the big leather chair beside it are both polished and uncluttered. Everything else in the room belongs here: a music stand, records and sheet music, the Victrola that Ben must have carried upstairs.

Ellen smiles. "You've kept this room so nice! So you still play?"

Eva glances around nervously.

Ellen smiles again. "I know why you brought me up here—to play a duet, didn't you? Like we used to?"

Eva nods.

"Come on, then." Ellen pulls out the bench and sits down.

Eva watches cautiously.

"Please." Ellen leans over and pulls the edge of

her cape. "One duet? Like we used to play?"

Eva shuffles to the door. Closing it she turns the key in the lock. Then she returns and sits on the piano bench next to Ellen.

Ellen's hands go to the keyboard. "What shall we start with? *Here we go up to Wunderlich, Wunderlich, Wunderlich*—remember?" Ellen, pressing down the keys, winces at the tinny sound. Reaching over gently, she lifts Eva's right hand to the keyboard.

Eva insists on guiding her own gloved hand. When she plays, the melody is off by one note.

"That's okay," Ellen says, playing it the correct way again. "You'll get it if we practice." Facing Eva, she laughs shyly. "I feel so much better now. I'm so glad you brought me up here. I was starting to think maybe you—didn't really want me here." She sits back. "Hey, I just got an idea. I have to go home now—my mother's expecting me for supper—but tomorrow's Saturday. I don't have to go to the hospital, so I can come and visit you most of the day. I'll bring food. We can play the piano again and clean up a little bit, and—" She pauses. "How about if I bring somebody with me?"

Eva stiffens. "No strangers!"

"Not a stranger," Ellen says. "It's a girl friend of mine who admires you."

"They all did, you know."

"Yes—I know. May I bring her? There's a lot to do around here. An extra person could help. Is it okay?"

72

Eva nods skeptically.

"Good." Ellen slides off the bench. "I've really got to go now." She looks around once more at the neatly arranged furniture. "Does Alicia take care of this room?"

Eva's penciled eyebrows arch. "No one comes in here. Only—" She points first to herself and then to Ellen.

"Oh," Ellen says. "Well, maybe you could call Alicia tonight about all that mail downstairs. Do you think you could?"

"Yes, yes," Eva says impatiently. "Come. Play again."

"Not now. We'll play tomorrow, okay?"

Eva beckons her.

Ellen shakes her head. "I'm coming back in the morning, remember? With food and my friend—"

"They all leave," Eva whispers in a faraway voice.

"Not me," Ellen says. "*I swear.*" She hovers at the bench. "Don't think I'm leaving because of anything you did. You don't think that, do you? I'm going now so I can help you tomorrow." She lays her hand timidly on Eva's cape. "See you then?"

"*Stay.*" Eva's eyes implore her.

"I can't," Ellen says· apologetically. "Don't you believe me, that I'll come back?"

"They all go," Eva whispers again.

"Wait a second." Ellen lifts her hand from the cape. "How's this?" She tugs at her finger. "This is my new ring, see? I just got it for my birthday. Isn't it nice? I'm going to leave it with you, to show you I'm coming back. How's that?" Smiling, she pushes it, as gently as she can, over the leather glove, onto Eva's little finger.

Eva stares at the clear, pale, bluish-green stone. She holds her hand up to the light.

Ellen nods. "Pretty, isn't it?"

Eva's lips curl in the hint of a smile.

"You believe me then, that I'm coming back? We can say good-bye until tomorrow?"

Eva nods distractedly.

While she has the chance, Ellen walks away from the piano, turns the key in the lock, and opens the door of the music room. Thank heaven. Eva isn't trying to stop her. Breathing quickly, Ellen hurries down the steps so fast that she catches her foot on something. The telephone! Buried until now under a pile of papers at the base of the stairs. Picking up the receiver, Ellen's suspicion is confirmed. No dial tone. Dead silence. No wonder Eva hasn't called Alicia.

Eager now to share all this with someone else, so she'll know she hasn't imagined it, Ellen makes her way through the living room and half runs to the bus stop. If she's lucky, the bus to the Square will come along in a few minutes and Josie will still be hanging out at Giese's.

eleven

"What'd you tell your mother, El?" Josie asks.

Ellen, coming back from the pay phone, slips into the booth. "Nothing—yet. I can't tell her on the phone. I told her, 'I'm at Giese's Grill with Josie. Can I eat here and sleep over at her house?' and she said, 'fine,' so no problem about tomorrow."

"That's cool. Let's order." Josie signals the waitress. "A BLT, Trudy—hold the T—and a large Coke."

"A medium cheeseburger," Ellen says. "And a glass of iced tea, please." She looks at Josie. "For a second I had this urge to say to my mother, 'Eva's in terrible shape. You've got to help.'"

Josie casts up her eyes. "Her and your grandparents? That'd be like asking the Three Bears to help Goldilocks."

Ellen is silent for a second. "It's just that my mother would know how to do things like get the electricity back on."

Josie's leg bumps against the booth. "Electricity isn't the point, Ellen. You're too hung up on *electricity*."

"You didn't see the place!"

"Don't remind me! Why didn't you wait? Okay, look—so long as you've come to your senses, finally." Josie's bracelets clink on the table. "You get my point at least, about electricity? Did the Pilgrims have it? Do the Riegel twins have electricity at the fancy camp they're at, that costs over *one thousand dollars per kid*?"

"Don't be stupid," Ellen says. "That's only for eight weeks, and they're choosing to live like that."

"Eva's choosing. She's one of the few people around who *is*. Look at everybody else, tied down to getting rid of their crabgrass and buying a new car every year. Are they happy?"

"What makes you think Eva's happy?" Ellen asks.

"She does whatever she feels like doing."

"By herself. She's always alone."

"We'll change that."

Ellen shakes her head. "Even if we went every day— She needs somebody to take care of her."

"She's a beautiful person, Ellen. Leave her be!"

"What about *safety*?"

"Nobody's safe for sure." Josie looks up at the ceiling. "We could be getting diseases right this minute from the asphalt up there."

"Asbestos," Ellen says.

"Asphalt, asbestos." Josie shrugs. "Or *ptomaine*," she says as Trudy serves them. "I could die of ptomaine poisoning tonight."

"Then I'd have to go to Eva's by myself tomorrow, wouldn't I?"

Josie blinks. "Are you trying to tell me something? Would you rather go by yourself again?"

Ellen shakes her head. "No. I want you to come. I want you to see what it's like. But not just to say, 'Oh, wow, this is something else!' I want you to come because she needs *help*."

"Well, sure. We're bringing her food, aren't we?"

Ellen nods. "We'll shop tonight. I stopped and took money out of the bank. First thing in the morning we'll make sandwiches." She toys with her cheeseburger, pushes it away. "Eva's so sad, Josie. Maybe it'll be better with you there. Maybe I'm too gloomy or something."

"You are." Josie chews noisily. "Don't worry, I'll cheer her up. I'm good with people like her. One time in New York City I talked to this—"

"I know."

Josie crams the last bite of sandwich into her mouth. "How come you aren't eating your burger?"

"I'm not hungry. Take it."

"Thanks. Hey," she says, "I didn't get a chance to

tell you before. I saw Ben and Buddha today. They don't have to work tomorrow night and they want to know if we can go out. What do you think? Will we be back from Eva's in time?"

"I guess so," Ellen says. "I have to see Ben. I have his bathing suit."

"His bathing suit?"

"Yeah, he dropped it on my porch."

Josie grabs her wrist. "Oh my God. What did you *do*?"

"He wasn't wearing it!"

"Oh." She pauses. "I think he likes you. He was asking me things."

"What things?"

"What hours you work, stuff like that." Josie tilts her head. "What do you think of him?"

"He's nice. I've known him for ages."

"So have I, but I never really noticed him till he pierced his ear. It's such a great statement. Isn't it amazing—somebody does something different, you notice them?" She fluffs up her hair with her fingertips. "Think I should frost my ends?"

"Not now, Josie. Not tonight. Come on," Ellen says. "Let's get going to the supermarket."

twelve

"Did you try this kind yet?" Josie offers the plate to Eva again. "Egg and green pepper, crabmeat, cream cheese, and watercress. Not my idea of great sandwiches, frankly, but Ellen said you like them."

Ellen looks at the blob of mayonnaise on Eva's glove. "Wouldn't you like to take your gloves off to eat, Grandma Eva?"

"No, no." Eva picks up another sandwich and eats it hungrily. The flowers on her straw hat bob up and down as she chews.

Josie keeps offering the plate. "Go on, don't be bashful. They're so *small*. I wanted to make them normal size, but Ellen said they had to be triangles with the crusts off. Fan-*cy*!"

Eva, looking suspiciously at Josie, transfers the sandwiches one by one onto her own paper plate.

"Great," Josie says. "That's what they're there for." Sitting back on the cement bench, she sighs. "I love it. I *love* this house. I'm dying to get a look at the inside. You've got a fantastic place here."

Eva puts one sandwich in her mouth and another in her canvas bag.

"Good idea." Josie nods. "You never know when you might be out somewhere and get hungry."

"*Josie*," Ellen says sharply. She turns to Eva. "You don't have to do that. We can bring more food tomorrow." She clears her throat. "Some more iced tea?" She pours. Eva has a cream-cheese mustache, Ellen sees, and a bit of egg salad stuck to her cheek.

"I love your rings," Josie says, touching Eva's gloved hand.

Eva pulls back.

"This one Ellen gave you," Josie goes on. "Where did the others come from?"

Ellen wishes Josie would shut up.

Eva, watching Josie warily, reaches for another sandwich.

Josie shakes her wrist. "I'm more into bracelets myself. My grandmother says I look like a street-walker with my bangles and beads, but I don't care. I wish my grandmother had some of the style *you* have. Unfortunately she's super ordinary. She lives in one of those senior citizen developments where they shoot you on sight if you're under fifty-five."

80

Ellen, trying not to look, sees lipstick mixing with egg salad as Eva chews.

"My grandmother's got this little house behind a wire fence that looks just like seventeen thousand *other* little houses," Josie continues. "What *I* love is originality, like this house. And I think it's so great that you still drive," she says to Eva. "My grandmother gave up her car, so the only way she can get around is in this blue mini-bus that says 'Twilight Years Transport,' or something like that." Josie pats Eva's arm. "You're keeping your freedom. I admire that."

Eva blinks. "Who is she?" she asks Ellen.

"My friend Josie," Ellen says evenly. "You said I could bring her, remember? She's wanted to meet you for a long time. I've told her all about you. How we used to play games and piano duets—"

"Don't tell!" Eva says hoarsely. Agitated, she bounces out of her seat. Bits of egg fall from her cape.

"Wait!" Ellen calls. "There's dessert."

Eva, narrowing her eyes at Josie, turns her back on them.

Ellen jumps up and takes a container of strawberries from under the bench. "Please sit down, Grandma Eva. We brought you strawberries. Remember how you and Alicia and I always had strawberries?"

Eva inspects the container and sits down again. She waits with her hand out while Ellen spoons berries into a clean paper cup. Then, reaching eagerly for the berries, she drops the plastic spoon that Ellen has given her into her canvas bag and shoves her hand directly into the cup. After she has popped the berries one by one into her mouth, Eva tilts the cup to her lips so that a trickle of juice runs down her neck. She rubs the wet place with her sticky glove.

"That's okay. Don't worry about it," Josie says. "Enjoy your food, that's the main thing. Here, have some more."

Josie fills Eva's cup again. This time the juice splashes down the front of her cape.

"Let me get that." Ellen dabs with a paper napkin.

Josie watches. "I'm thinking of getting a used fur," she says offhandedly. "Would you mind telling me where you got yours, Eva?"

"*Josie!*" Ellen says hostilely. "Let's go inside now. We're going to carry out some of the newspapers, okay, Grandma Eva? Come on," she whispers to Josie. "It's getting late. Ben and Buddha are going to be waiting."

Josie dances ahead of them toward the French doors. But Eva turns and walks down the steps of the porch.

"Where are you going?" Ellen asks. She watches as Eva goes around the back of the house past the summer kitchen, where Ellen remembers chasing Toby in and out through his little door. Eva takes

82

the path by the gazebo and disappears into the woods. Suddenly Ellen recalls what's back there.

"Aren't you guys coming?" Josie calls.

Ellen joins Josie in the living room. "I think Eva's gone to the outhouse. There used to be one, at least. I was wondering how she managed without plumbing."

"I told you she knows what she's doing. Man!" Josie makes a kissing sound. "I love it. *I love this room!* Look at the works of art in this place!" She struggles to lift a small statue.

"Who's that?" Ellen asks.

Josie examines the statue. "Some guy named Franz . . . Schubert," she says. "Who's he?"

"A composer. Put it back, Josie."

Josie puts the statue back on a table and opens the desk. "Incredible. This is the mail you told me about?"

"Yes. Be careful it doesn't fall out."

Josie picks up a packet of letters, which are tied with a ribbon.

"Come on, Josie, don't touch anything."

"Hey, here's one from 'Fred'. Isn't that your father?"

"Let me see it."

"Take them." Josie hands over the pack. "All in the family, right?"

Ellen hesitates for a second and then slips the letters into her pocket. "*Now* what are you doing?" she asks.

Josie is opening the doors of the big metal wardrobe at the foot of the stairs. "Oh, wow!"

"What?"

"Look at the clothes!" Stepping into the wardrobe, Josie gathers skirts and gowns in both arms and buries her face in them. "Incredible!"

Ellen recognizes some of the same outfits she dressed up in years ago.

Josie's head emerges. "I went to that second-hand place on Main Avenue and they had *nothing* this great. Do you think she'd loan me something, Ellen?"

"Josie, I don't think—"

Josie, meanwhile, slips a beaded top over her T-shirt. "On second thought, I'll offer to buy. She can use the money, right?" She examines herself in a mirror on the wall. "How does this look on me?"

"*Josie*—" Ellen breaks off suddenly.

Eva, back in the room, is shuffling toward them. Bits of dried grass are clinging to her cape.

"I hope you don't mind," Ellen says to her nervously. "Josie was . . . admiring your things."

Eva fixes her eyes on Josie. Her lips twitch.

Josie steps into the wardrobe to reach for a hanger. "I was just saying to Ellen, if you ever want to get rid of any of these things—"

Eva's face contorts. "No strangers take my things!"

"Josie's no stranger," Ellen calls out, but her words are lost in the confusion, as Eva, with surprising force, gives Josie a shove that sends her reeling backward into the clothes.

"Stop!" Ellen says, unable to believe what's happening.

Slamming the wardrobe door, Eva already has the key in her hand.

Ellen hears the click of the key in the lock and sees the expression of satisfaction on Eva's face.

"Hey!" Josie's muffled cry comes from inside the wardrobe.

"No strangers," Eva mutters, heading toward the French doors.

"Come back, Grandma Eva!" Ellen follows her.

"Very funny, Ellen." Josie is banging now. Metallic rumbles, like the sound of thunder in a play, fill the room.

Ellen hovers between the wardrobe and the porch. "Wait, Josie, I'll get the key!"

"Some joke. Come on, before I pass out!"

Ellen, tripping over a piece of lumber, weaves her way through the rubble toward the doors. "Grandma Eva!" she shouts again. And then her voice fails her as she stands on the steps and watches Eva back a maroon car out of the driveway and chug off down the boulevard.

thirteen

"Josie?" Ellen rattles the handle so that the whole wardrobe vibrates. Sweat is trickling over her temples and down her neck. "Josie?" She stops rattling. "*Josie!*"

Josie's voice sounds hollow. "Open up, if you want me to talk."

"I *can't* open up. She drove off. She drove away with the key!"

For a moment the only noise inside the wardrobe is a single *clunk*. "What do you mean?"

"It's no joke, Josie. Eva locked you in there, and now she's gone. In her car. What should I do?"

"You're kidding. It wasn't you—?"

Ellen leans her forehead against the crack where the doors of the wardrobe meet. "It was *her*, Josie.

You made her mad. I tried to warn you."

"Mad about what?"

"You touched her things. You asked if she wanted to get rid of them."

Josie's elbow bangs the side of the wardrobe. "So why didn't she just say no? My feelings wouldn't have been hurt."

"Because—" Ellen stops. The truth hits her with the force of a shove. "*Because she's not normal,* Josie. You can't pretend she is. You can't treat her like she is!"

"Hell, I was just trying to be nice."

"I know, I know, but—" Ellen jiggles the handle again. "Are you okay? Are you getting any air? Some must be coming in through that crack." She runs her hand along the top of the wardrobe. "And through that vent. Are you passing out?"

"Not yet." Josie's voice sounds tinny. "Where'd she go?"

"How should I know? Do you still think it's so great that she's a free spirit? She could be gone for hours. What should I do, call my mother?"

"We'd never hear the end of it."

"You'd rather suffocate?"

"Yes." She pauses. "Ellen?"

"What?"

"You swear this isn't a joke? She isn't standing right there with the key?"

"What do you think I came here for, to play games?"

"You said she liked to."

"A long time ago. So did I, but not like *this*. This is no game. Aren't you getting claustrophobia?"

"Clothestrophobia!" Josie lets out a hoot. "Yeah, fear of old clothes!" The wardrobe echoes with Josie's tinny laughter. She beats a tattoo on the inside of the door. "Oh, man, can you believe this? One minute I'm admiring the place, and the next I'm a prisoner in a clothes closet! Hey, Ellen, it's dark in here, you know? And hot. Whew! How about a little air freshener?" Josie shouts. "Clothes up to my nose! What are Ben and Buddha going to think?"

"I don't know. They're probably there already, waiting for us. I think I'd better go get a locksmith."

"Hey, don't *go*."

"How else am I going to get you out?"

"Wait." The wardrobe creaks as Josie shifts positions. "Try the doors again. One, two, three—on three, you pull and I'll kick."

Ellen, bracing herself, pulls as hard as she can.

The wardrobe quivers.

"Ow, my foot!" Josie yells. The doors hold firm.

"How about a crowbar or something?" Josie calls out. "There's one of everything in this room, isn't there?"

Ellen looks at the junk around her. "Only things nobody *needs*. Do you think she'd have something *useful*?"

"Hey, don't get on Eva's case." Josie's voice is faint and far away. "If she's really so bad off, then we've got to try to understand her."

Ellen rests her cheek on the cool metal door. "That's very forgiving of you, Josie. But you see what I mean now, how she can't be left alone? I'm going to call my mother."

"Don't leave me!"

"I'll call from the next house—from the Riegels'." She puts her mouth close to the crack between the doors. "I thought you were okay. You can breathe, can't you?"

"Not as good now. The heat's getting to me. I feel weak."

Ellen tries to see inside, but the crack is too fine. "Let me go quick, and—"

"Don't go! Use the phone."

"There isn't any phone!"

"*Don't go*, Ellen. It's getting bad in here. I'm soaked through, Ellen. I'm breathing my own carbon monoxide."

"Carbon *di*oxide."

"Monoxide, dioxide—get me out of here, Ellen. I'm passing out, I swear. It's like a coffin. My grandfather was buried in one made of metal, just like this. Please get me out, Ellen."

Looking around desperately, Ellen grabs a hammer from the top of a pile of papers. She taps gingerly on the lock. "I'm afraid of breaking the handle off. It might be worse that way. Josie?"

Josie doesn't answer.

"Don't kid around, Josie. Answer me!"

The only sound is a faint metallic creak.

"Josie!" Ellen's breath is as shallow as if she's the one inside. "I'm going next door to the phone, Josie. If they're not home, I'll try every house until I find someone who is. I'll get the police if I have to. Just don't panic, okay? Please don't give up, Josie!" Afraid of the silence, Ellen doesn't wait any longer. She dashes as fast as she can across the living room and out the French doors.

Her body is clammy. Her chest pounds. And then, as she takes the porch steps in one leap, she hears a car pulling into the driveway. "I knew you'd come back!" she's about to call, until she realizes that it isn't an old beat-up maroon car at all, but a VW squareback.

fourteen

"Brace it, Buddha, so it doesn't move!" Buddha plants himself behind the wardrobe while Ben rams the jack from the VW into the space between the doors.

"Everything's going to be okay, Josie," Ellen says, trying to convince herself.

Ben applies leverage, the wardrobe shimmies slightly, and the doors spring open with a harsh crack.

"Josie!" Ellen holds the doors open.

Josie, pale and drenched with sweat, tumbles out. Ben catches her. "You okay?"

Her chest heaving, she nods.

Ellen is half laughing, half crying. "Why didn't you answer me?"

"I *panicked*." Josie, yanking off Eva's beaded top, fans her face with both hands. "I couldn't talk! Fresh air!" She bounds through the living room to the porch.

Ellen and Ben follow her. Buddha lingers, surveying the room.

Josie throws herself onto the cement bench, where the remnants of lunch are still scattered. "Oh, God!" Lying on her back, looking up at the sky, she pulls her sticky T-shirt away from her body. "It was just like being buried alive, I swear."

"Are you sure you're okay?" Ellen asks, her voice cracking.

Josie pushes back the hair that is plastered to her forehead. "As soon as I breathe some *air*."

"Here, maybe something to drink—" Ellen grabs a cup of iced tea and holds it to her lips.

Josie, raising herself on one elbow, drinks until the cup is empty. "More." The pulse in her throat throbs.

Ellen fills the cup again. "I think we should take you to a doctor."

"No! Just let me breathe!" Josie flings out her arms.

Ellen moves back reluctantly and crouches on the floor of the porch next to Ben. "How did you know to come?" she asks faintly.

"After we waited awhile, I figured we should take a look. Why the hell did Eva do it?"

Ellen covers her face. "Because she's crazy. Josie annoyed her," Ellen whispers, "and that's how Eva dealt with it. I was so scared, Ben! I'll tell you later." She raises her head slowly. "Where's Buddha?"

"Still nosing around in there."

"Let's go," Ellen says. "She might come back, and I don't want to see her."

Ben meets her eyes. "Nothing's gone right, huh?"

She shakes her head.

"Josie, you feel good enough to get up?" Ben asks.

Rolling over on her side, she starts to raise herself. "Yeah."

"Where do you want to go?" Ben asks them.

Josie sits up. "Someplace *cool*."

"How about down by the creek in Palmer Park?" Ben says.

Josie fans herself again. "Excellent. Get Buddha out here."

"Lightner!" Ben goes into the living room and comes out dragging Buddha by the shirttail.

"Hell, this is cruel," Buddha says. "First interesting thing I've seen since I hit town, and you're cutting me short. This place ought to be open to the public. Hey, Josie, how's it going?"

"Not too bad. Just a little brain damage, but who'll be able to tell, right? Thanks for coming—no kidding—both of you."

Buddha shrugs. "Forget it. It's made my day." He

turns to Ellen. "How come you didn't *tell* me about your grandmother? You going to introduce us sometime?"

"No."

"Why not? You're not ashamed, are you?"

"Not of *her*."

"Funny!" Buddha swings the jack in one hand and the car keys in the other. "Hey, can't we take the beer and blankets and go out in the woods here?"

"*No*," Ellen says. "Maybe I'd better go right home."

Josie gets up. "Ellen, don't! You're too tense. So am I. We need to unwind. Let's go to Palmer like Ben said. All I want to do is jump in the creek and sit there."

Buddha nods. "Me, too, with a brew in each hand."

"Come," Ben urges her. "To the park first. I'll take you home whenever you want."

Ellen hesitates. "Okay."

Buddha, first to the driveway, examines the two remaining maroon cars. "Oh my God, a 1947 Studebaker," he calls. "You know what a collector's item that is? And a '56 Lincoln! Too bad she let 'em get so beat. Look—flat tires on both. Hey, I know somebody who'd make her a good offer."

"Come *on*, Buddha." Ben pulls him by the shirt again.

Buddha, tearing himself away reluctantly, opens the doors on both sides of the VW and gets in behind the wheel. "How'd your grandmother get like this, anyway?"

Ellen is in the back seat now, next to Ben. "I'd tell you if I knew."

Buddha starts up the motor. "She was always off-the-wall?"

"I didn't used to think so," Ellen says quietly.

He backs onto the boulevard. "But this time it's too much, huh?"

Ellen doesn't answer.

Josie's hair blows wildly as they pick up speed. "I forgive her, Ellen. Tell her when you see her."

Buddha looks at Ellen in the rearview mirror. "I sympathize, you know? I know what a pain it is to put up with wacko relatives." He stops at a light. "Did I ever tell you about my cousin? He can't stand *germs*, this guy. He brings his own silverware and stuff when he comes to visit. Everything's marked with tape. Once I pretended to use his toothbrush. He didn't brush his teeth for six months after that. They were green."

"So's the light," Ben says.

Buddha steps on the gas and turns onto East Main Avenue. "He's nothing, though," Buddha goes on, "compared to his father." He weaves into the fast lane. "My uncle's a cat freak. Not my Windsor uncle—another uncle. He's got twenty-five cats. You go into his house holding your nose—a wall-to-wall sandbox. Once one of 'em clawed me through my clothes." Buddha hunches over the wheel. "Alfred Hitchcock's next movie was gonna be about my uncle's cats, but he died. Hitchcock, that is. My uncle's still kicking."

Josie looks at him sideways. "You're kidding."

"I'll swear on that case of beer back there! Feel it, Bernhauser. Is it still cold?"

Ben reaches behind the seat. "Yeah."

"Give me one, will you? Help yourselves."

Ben pulls off the tab and hands a can to Buddha. "Anybody else?"

Josie thrusts her hand between the seats. "Yes, *please*."

Ellen stirs. "I'll take one, too." She takes a sip and feels the cold bitterness in her throat.

"Well, we got off to a hell of a start," Buddha says, "but I have a hunch this is going to be a good party. I'm finally going to teach you guys to play Quarters. You bounce this quarter, see, and if it lands in the glass of beer, you point to somebody, and they've got to chug-a-lug it down. Here's to a great blast." He raises the can. Beer sloshes onto the seat as the VW rumbles over the bridge.

"By the way," Buddha goes on, "you think your grandmother's a case, and my uncle? We had this family down the block from us, the Zolneys. Skinny old Mr. Zolney and his two big fat daughters. None of 'em ever went out of their house in thirty years, at least. A kid used to leave them groceries on their doorstep every couple of days."

Buddha turns off the bridge at the park exit. "Okay. So one day there's this *smell* in the neighborhood, right? Well, the cops decide to check it out." Buddha slows down as they reach the tree-lined park drive. "The cops ring the bell, knock, and what do you think they find? Garbage piled higher than your grandmother's junk. They're up to their eyeballs in garbage," Buddha says, tossing an empty beer can out of the window. "Get the picture?"

Josie nods. Ellen tilts her can of beer and swallows quickly.

" 'Disgusting!' That's what the cops say," Buddha goes on. " 'Who owns this house?' "

" 'Our father,' the daughters tell the cops. 'But he can't be disturbed. He's in the bathroom.' "

" 'We'll wait,' the cops say." Buddha slows down at the park entrance. "So the cops wait and wait, and finally they decide something's fishy, so they bust into the bathroom, and guess what they see?" Buddha glances toward the back seat. "This *skeleton* in the bathtub, with little bits of Old Man Zolney still hanging on for flavor! How about that? Right on my street!" Buddha pulls onto the shoulder of the road by the creek. "You think we've got loonies in *our* families? Hell, compared to Zolneys, we've got solid citizens."

The VW stops. Ellen and Ben look at each other.

"Hey, don't just sit there. We're here!" Buddha

throws open the door. "Bring the beer, Bernhauser. Forget about crazies. It's time for a nice healthy game like Quarters."

"Bad shot, Ellen. Bottoms up!" Buddha, watching Ellen take a swig of beer, grabs the quarter and moves backward onto the grass. "My turn. Watch this—a long shot." He arches the coin toward the can without a top, which is set in the middle of the blanket. "Nuts!" he says as the quarter bounces off the side of the can. He guzzles beer. "Okay, Josie, you're on."

Josie tosses and the quarter flies over the can into Ellen's lap. "Oh, no!" Josie moans. "It's not my day." She drinks. "Ben's turn."

Ben aims. There is a solid *plunk* as the quarter lands in the can. Ben shrugs. "Nothing to it."

"Not for you, maybe." Ellen wrinkles her nose as Buddha hands her the coin. "Do I have to keep going?"

Buddha's eyes glimmer behind his glasses. "Yeah, unless—here's something we did up in Maine to make the game last longer. It's Ellen's turn, right? Okay. Instead of zipping the quarter right off, she gets a choice. She can answer a personal question we ask her and get by her turn. Or, if the question's too personal, she can still decide to throw. What do you say?"

Ellen pauses. "Okay, ask me a question."

98

"What are you thinking right now about your grandmother?" Ben asks.

Buddha snorts. "That's not personal!"

"Yes, it is." Ellen looks at Ben. "I feel awful about her. I almost hate her—that's the truth."

Josie rises to her knees. "How can you?"

"I can't help it. Everything that used to be interesting about her is too much now. Too much makeup, too many rings. And that's the least of it. I used to like the kooky things she did, but now they're *too* kooky."

"Would you rather have a grandmother like mine?" Josie asks.

"Josie," Ellen says agitatedly, "what does it take to wake you up? What if Ben and Buddha hadn't come a little while ago? What if I hadn't been able to find anybody to get you out of that stupid wardrobe? Don't be so dense!"

Josie blinks. "I'm not dense, I'm sympathetic!"

"Okay, okay." Buddha raises his hand. "On with the game. No question for me. I'll throw." Standing at the edge of the blanket, he flips the quarter. "Damn, so close!" Tilting back his head, he finishes off a beer in a few gulps. "Bernhauser, you're up."

"I'll take a question," Ben says.

Ellen's head feels light. The trees in this isolated spot by the creek suddenly seem to be moving like a speeded-up movie set on reverse. "Why do you wear the earring, Ben?" she hears herself asking him.

Ben touches it with his fingertips. "It's my plumage," he says with a grin. "Ever hear of the male of the species attracting the female with his plumage?"

"Peacocks do that," Ellen says.

Buddha smirks. "Hell. I'd be worried about who might get the wrong message and follow me home."

Ben shrugs. "Anybody'd be better than who you got following you now, man—*nobody*." He turns to Ellen. "How do you like the way it looks? Tell the truth."

"I like it," she says. "I do. Most of the time I forget it's there. Then I see it and I think—yeah, I like it."

Josie smiles. "I think it's beautiful, Ben. It's a real statement. Plus, it's very sexy."

Buddha looks at her. "Yeah? No kidding? You think an earring on a guy is sexy? You think so too, Ellen?"

She nods.

"Bernhauser?"

"What?"

"Think you could get me one of those things?"

"Sure. Tell you what, lend me your car sometime, and in exchange I'll give you an earring."

"It's a deal. Hey!" Buddha raises his beer can.

"The game! Whose turn is it? Want a question, Josie?"

She shakes her head. "Forget it. I know what *you'd* ask. I'd rather take my chances." Throwing underhanded, she misses and takes a long swallow of beer.

Buddha points. "Ellen!"

"I'll try another question."

"Okay," Buddha says, "I get to ask this one. And just to show you my mind isn't where Josie thinks it is—Ellen, did you ever swipe anything? Forget candy bars and stuff like that. I'm talking about something big."

Hesitating a moment, Ellen nods.

"What'd you rip off?"

Ellen, looking from Josie to Ben, sees them waiting expectantly, and a wave of nausea comes over her. It's the beer, or tension from before. Or this new disgust with Eva that's making her feel so rotten. "I took something a long time ago, but I don't feel like talking about it," she says. "Give me the quarter." Flinging it carelessly so that it sails over the blanket, she grabs the nearest can of beer and drinks without taking a breath.

"Hey." Ben lifts the can out of her hand. "What do you say we go home now?"

"Yes," Ellen says. "Let's." Struggling to get up off the blanket, she discovers that the only way she can make it is to hang on to Ben and let him help her.

Buddha drives out of the park onto Palmer Avenue. "Pathetic, breaking up a beer blast while it's still light out."

Josie's eyes are shut. "What do you mean, light?"

Buddha shakes his head. "If you two hadn't had such a rough day, I'd be sore at you. We'll finish Quarters another time. Where's your house, Dohrmann? Where do I turn?"

Ellen tries to sit up.

"Bright Avenue," Ben says. "Make a left at the corner."

The sloshing in Ellen's stomach is worse now. Her head is pounding. Slipping on the seat, she lets herself go limp against Ben's shoulder.

"Here?" Buddha jams on the brake.

"Yeah, second house," Ben says. "You're going to have to let us out on your side. Come on, Ellen, we're here."

Ellen steps cautiously onto the curb.

"Thanks for the ride," Ben calls. "Don't wait for me. Take Josie home. She's had it."

The cracks in the sidewalk rise to meet Ellen as she walks up the path. The porch light dips and whirls like a sparkler. *Thank Ben,* she tells herself. Give him his bathing suit. But the churning in her stomach is suddenly so wild that she has just enough time to throw her head over the railing and let the warm, sour stream shoot out. Leaning against the rail, supported by Ben, she heaves again.

"It's okay," Ben says. "Get it out."

"I feel so *awful*." She shudders, wiping her wet face with the back of her hand.

"Get it all out," he repeats soothingly.

And she does, finally, after a few more heaves that leave her breathless and aching.

"You're sure you can make it?" Ben asks in the downstairs hall.

Ellen holds on to the banister. A loose strand of hair clings to her cheek. Her nose is running. "Yes. Thanks for everything. I—"

"Don't talk. You'll need all you've got for your mother. Sure you don't want me to walk you up the steps?"

"I'm sure." She hangs onto the banister with both hands.

"I'll call you tomorrow afternoon. You're going to sleep late, I have a feeling."

"Ben?" She covers the stain on her blouse with her hand. "Don't watch me go up the steps, okay?"

He hesitates. "Okay. Good night. Get a good sleep."

fifteen

The door closes and suddenly the long, dark stairway looks as scary to Ellen as it did when she was little. The thing in the corner at the top is only an umbrella stand, she assures herself. Hand-over-hand on the banister, she pulls herself up. Weights seem to drag her backward, though, and her head pounds again to the beat of a song out of tune.

Halfway up the stairs she stops. What will she tell her mother? Everything. *I'm drunk*, she'll begin. *And I didn't listen to you—I went to Eva's.* Suddenly she can't wait to explain. Groping in her bag for her house key, she decides to ring the bell instead. She rings, then knocks. Where's her mother?

Ellen fumbles for the key now. Finally, guiding it

with concentration, she opens the door to the apartment. "Mother!" she calls. "Mom?"

The living room, spookily quiet, reminds her of a still life painting in blues and grays. No lamps are lit. No sound comes from the bedroom or the kitchen. "Mother?" she calls again. A shade rattles faintly. Should she call Nonie to find out where her mother is? No, not in this condition.

Ellen stumbles to the couch and, focusing her eyes as well as she can, she looks again at the silent living room. The coffee table, neat and polished. The photographs on the mantel: her father, Nonie and Grandpa, her mother. Where is her mother? And then she notices a sheet of paper propped between two pictures. Muscles aching, she pulls herself up off the couch and reaches for it.

Dear Ellen,

I tried to call you at Josie's all afternoon. I've left messages everywhere, but if you get this one first, the news is that Grandpa wasn't feeling well today, so Dr. Lindeman told us to bring him in to the hospital as a precaution. Don't worry. It's not an emergency. I may be home late, so you go on to bed.

Love,
Mother

She rereads the note and then folds it slowly. What it tells her is that Grandpa will die. If not now, then soon. Grandpa who read comics to her and taught her to ride a bicycle. Grandpa who still calls her Ellie and tells her silly jokes but in a way treats her more like an adult than anybody else does. Grandpa who's never in his life done anything mean or crazy. So sad. The people who are always nice to you, you take for granted, and the ones you try especially hard to show your love to, don't appreciate it. Is there still enough time, she wonders, to let Grandpa know what he's meant to her?

Retreating to the couch, Ellen collapses on it. Nothing is going right. Maybe she should have stayed clear of Eva. She *will*, from now on. Her head still pounding, Ellen thinks back over the events of the afternoon. Sitting up suddenly, she thrusts her hand in her pocket. The letters from Eva's desk! She switches on the light on the end table. Here they are. She watches flakes flutter to her lap as she takes them out. One, two, three envelopes.

Ellen lingers first over a note in large, careful handwriting. Written by her own father when he was a boy, writing to Eva from boarding school.

> *Dear Mother,*
> *Thank you for the birthday present. It's just what I wanted. I would like to stay with you at Christmas, but Dad already arranged for me to go to Switzerland. I will come see you before I go.*
>
> *Love,*
> *Fred*

She keeps examining it, as if rereading could by some miracle reveal this shadowy person whose looks and blood and name she has. What did he really want to do over Christmas vacation, she wonders, go with his father or stay with Eva?

Realizing that she'll never know, Ellen shuffles on to the next piece of paper. She smiles at the large print in red crayon. How old was she when she wrote this note to Eva? Seven at the most.

> *Dear Grandma Eva,*
> *I will tell my mother I have to come early this Saturday and then you and me will go to Wunderlich. O.K.? Don't worry, I won't tell.*
> > *I love you,*
> > *Ellen*

Ellen runs her finger over the waxy crayon. Did Eva encourage her to keep secrets from her mother? And is she imagining it, or did she and Eva talk sometimes about going far away—to Philadelphia or New York—without telling anyone? Ellen's memories of those afternoons are blurred, she realizes. Maybe things that seemed fine about Eva really weren't so good. One thing Ellen's sure of, though. When she wrote that *I love you* she meant it.

Ellen picks up the last of the three letters now and holds it up to the light.

My dearest Eva,

Alicia is to give you this note when it is safe—that is, when your father next goes out of town on business. Eva dear, it is too hard to explain why I went away from you. All I can say right now is that you must believe it was not your fault in the slightest. I still love you, even though there are many miles between us.

I understand from Alicia that your father has forbidden you to keep my photograph on your bureau or to use the music room where we spent happy times together. Until he relents, you will have to keep your memory of me alive in your heart.

I will try to write to you again, with Alicia's help. You'd best not answer, however, as your father will be angry if he finds out.

Your loving mother

Awful. *Awful* to have your mother go away. And to have your father forbid you even to look at her picture. So *that's* why Eva always acts as if there's something secret and naughty about the music room. A wave of melancholy washes over Ellen. Trying to figure out Eva is like putting together an enormous puzzle, with pieces scattered so wide no one will ever find them all. Folding the letter sadly and putting it back, Ellen sees a small newspaper clipping tucked in the envelope. The date is recent —last year.

MRS. ALICIA DONOVAN

Word was received by The Times *today of the death in Sarasota, Fla., of Alicia Shomer Donovan, age 88, formerly of Windsor. She is survived by a son, Rudolph, also of Sarasota. Mrs. Donovan was employed for many years in Windsor as a housekeeper.*

Ellen rests her head on the back of the couch. *They all leave,* Eva said yesterday. Yes, they all have: mother, husband, son, father, dog, housekeeper.

Stuffing the letters back in her pocket, Ellen buries her head in the couch cushion. Breathing is hard work, suddenly. All she sees is black. All she hears is the jangle of the shade against the window frame and the ghostly echo of Eva's off-key piano playing. Is there music somewhere, or is she imagining that, too? Ellen buries her face deeper. Grandpa will die, she thinks. Nonie soon after. One by one, everyone in her life will go, in one way or another. Ellen lifts her head and gasps for breath. Is this the kind of *alone* that Eva feels? Ellen is shaking all over. How does it start, anyway—craziness? Did Eva know when she crossed over the line? If so, was it anything like this—this shortness of breath, this confusion between what's real and what isn't, this fear that you're all alone forever?

Ellen sits shaking for several minutes until she can't stand it any longer. Getting up off the couch, she does the first thing that comes into her mind.

She runs down the hall, kicking off her sandals and throwing off her clothes on the way. Switching on the bathroom light, she turns on the shower full force and steps in. Cool water stings her skin and mixes with the tears that are streaming down her face.

She stays in the shower until the tears have stopped and her body is tingling. Shutting off the water, she dries herself carefully, as if her skin were bruised. Then—a quick dash and she's in bed. Eyes closed, she feels herself tumbling, as if she's shut up in a clothes dryer. Faces appear as she flip-flops: Buddha's, leering; Grandpa's, in pain; her mother's, sad but sympathetic. After that she falls into the kind of sleep where dream blurs into dream. In one, she watches helplessly as Eva's car goes off a cliff. In another, Ben, wearing his gold earring, slips into bed beside her.

When she wakes up in the morning her mother is sitting at the foot of her bed.

"How's Grandpa?" Ellen asks immediately.

"Better. He's resting."

"Can I see him?"

"I think so. Where were you yesterday?"

Ellen sits up, heavy-headed. She will tell her, but not now, not while Grandpa's still sick. "At the park with Josie," she says. "When can I see him?"

"This afternoon."

"Good," Ellen says, relieved that her mother isn't asking any more questions about yesterday.

110

sixteen

Ellen, getting off the elevator on Two West, feels dizzy for a moment from the smell of flowers and antiseptic. Ahead of her an old woman, walking slowly, hugs a pot of begonias in pink foil.

"Can I help with that?" Ellen asks, even though she's not in uniform.

"No thank you, dear, I have it."

Ellen hurries to the nurses' station. "Excuse me," she asks, "is it all right to visit my grandfather—Mr. Kreider?"

"It'll be fine—until his doctor comes."

Ellen goes on down the hall. She would take a few minutes to say hello to Mrs. Pfaff, but her door is closed.

She waits a moment outside Grandpa's room. His hair is all ruffled, she sees, and he's hooked up to a machine that is monitoring his heart. As she enters, he boosts himself up on the pillow.

"Hey, hey—Ellie!"

"Hi," she says shyly. Coming closer, she kisses him on the forehead.

"Don't be afraid," Grandpa says, clearing his throat. "Don't be afraid of this contraption. They're just trying to make me feel like a big shot."

Ellen looks at his damp face and at his hands, marked with small purple bruises. "How are you?"

His foot jerks under the sheet. "Still kickin'!"

"What do they say—the doctors?"

"They say, 'Don't try running a three-minute mile—not till tomorrow, at least.'" He reaches for her hand and squeezes it. "Come on, now, no pill talk. I get enough of that from your mother and Nonie." He shifts his position awkwardly. "What have *you* been doing?—that's what I want to know. Stayed over at Josie's, is that what I heard?"

Ellen pauses. "Yes. Friday night. Yesterday . . . we went to Palmer Park."

"With fellas, I bet."

"Yeah."

Grandpa smiles. "Who are the lucky son-of-a-guns?"

"Oh, Ben Bernhauser—you know, the boy who works at Zimmer's—and this other boy—"

"That was something, wasn't it?" Grandpa shakes

112

his head. "That hullabaloo in Zimmer's? Your Nonie's trying to say that that's what brought on my trouble here." He touches his chest. "I told her that's damned ridiculous! Now tell me something interesting. How's Josie?"

"Not so good."

"Oh? How's that?"

"We drank beer in the park yesterday."

"Uh-oh. How about you?"

"I'm okay—now."

Grandpa chuckles. "I shouldn't ask about before?"

"No."

"All right, not a word. Only on Two West I'll tell. It's lucky Sloan and Gunderson went home, or you'd never live it down."

"Have you met my other patients? How about Mrs. Pfaff?"

"Next door? No." Grandpa looks up slowly. "I never met the woman, Ellie, but I overheard. She passed away last night."

Ellen sits down on the edge of the bed. "Are you sure? Mrs. Pfaff? On Friday, I— She didn't seem—"

"Yes, well. You never know."

Ellen fixes her eyes on him.

"Hey, hey, don't worry about *me*." Grandpa raises himself again. "I'm coming out of here Tuesday, the latest. I've got a card game. Think I'd miss that?"

"Grandpa—" Ellen wishes he'd let her say what

113

she wants to say. "Last night when I came home and saw the note that you were sick, I felt so bad—"

"Don't drink so much beer from now on!"

"Grandpa," she begs, her eyes filling up, "don't joke."

"*Don't joke?*" he says, reaching for her hand again. "I have to, Ellie, don't you know? Otherwise I'd go bananas. How'd you like that?"

"I wouldn't." Ellen's tears overflow, and Grandpa, forgetting the monitor, pulls her toward him. She rests her head on his chest. "Joke all you want," she whispers.

Grandpa starts to give her a bear hug, the kind he gave her when she was little, but he stops.

Ellen sits up. "You're hurting yourself."

"No, no." Grandpa nods toward the foot of the bed. "It's just that this guy's jealous."

Ellen, turning around, sees Dr. Lindeman.

He comes to the side of the bed. "It'll take more than a hug to hurt Frank Kreider. This is Ellen?"

Grandpa nods. "Best medicine there is. She works here, you know. Weekdays, right on this floor."

"That's fine," Dr. Lindeman says. "Ellen, I'm going to give this young man the once-over. Would you mind stepping out for a minute?"

"I'm going now, Grandpa," she says.

He smiles. "One of those fellas waiting for you?"

"He's supposed to call."

"Be careful! See you tomorrow, Ellie. Thanks for coming."

"You're welcome. 'Bye, Grandpa."

Ellen walks by Mrs. Pfaff's room, where an aide is putting clean sheets on the bed. With her eyes straight ahead, Ellen hurries to the elevator. Next summer she'll work somewhere else.

Two West is noisier now than when she came in. Patients in robes are gathered around the window in the sun room. At the elevator two nurses, whispering animatedly, stop speaking when they see her. Suddenly Ellen can't wait to get out of here. She pushes the elevator button twice, as if that will bring it faster. The elevator comes, and Ellen is the first to step out when it reaches the lobby.

Following a red arrow, she heads for the same exit she took yesterday when she wanted to avoid Josie. *Call Josie,* she tells herself as she walks by the row of closed doors marked EKG, EEG. Halfway down the corridor she hears a commotion, and the peaceful Sunday afternoon is shattered by the wail of an ambulance directly outside in the Quiet Zone. Two cops hurry in through the Emergency Entrance. A group of curious onlookers has gathered just outside the waiting room.

Ellen, wondering what could be causing the stir, pushes in among the spectators. At first she can't see over the heads of the people in front of her.

115

Then one of the cops clears a path. "Stretcher coming this way!" he shouts.

Ellen moves to the fringe of onlookers, where she notices that several police cars are lined up outside. Voices drift through the open door.

"Can't they throw her out?" one officer calls to another.

"They don't want to get rough. They're waiting for a tow truck."

Ellen, leaving the other spectators, goes out the door, just before the attendants come through with a man on a stretcher.

Once outside, Ellen needs a moment to figure out what's going on. The ambulance is parked far from the entrance. Attendants are lifting another stretcher from it now, and beginning to lug it across the asphalt drive. All at once Ellen, glancing toward the Emergency Zone, understands what the problem is. She stares. The ambulance can't unload in its normal space by the Emergency Room because a car is in the way. Ellen's throat constricts. The car that is causing all the confusion is a maroon junk heap, and the driver is an old lady in a fur cape and a straw hat. One cop is trying to push the maroon car out of the Emergency Zone. Another cop is thrusting his hand in the open window as if to grab the steering wheel, but Eva rolls up the window and refuses to move the car an inch.

For a second Ellen feels strangely detached. This isn't really happening. Or if it is, it has nothing to do with her. She can just stand here against the wall, waiting for the outcome, as if this were a movie.

But already another siren can be heard, and a second ambulance is speeding into the lot behind the first. Cops, pedestrians, and ambulance staff scurry like ants around a demolished anthill. Another stretcher appears. Still another policeman shakes his fist at Eva.

Ellen would like to run home right now. She would like to meet Ben and hide out with him somewhere until she can forget about this. But she has a hunch that, in the midst of all the cops and doctors, she may be the one who stands the best chance of getting through to Eva.

Taking advantage of the noise and movement, Ellen slips unnoticed along the gray wall. The other spectators are behind her. The cops are preoccupied with the second ambulance. The officer who is pushing Eva's rear fender turns away for a moment, and Ellen, darting to the car, tries the door. It's locked. Pressing her face to the glass, she motions for Eva to let her in.

Eva opens the door, and Ellen jumps in on top of the bags and boxes on the front seat. She slams the door again and locks it. "Go!" she orders. And to Ellen's surprise, Eva, without any argument or delay, turns her key in the ignition, steps on the gas, and chugs out of the Emergency Zone away from Windsor General Hospital.

seventeen

Ellen turns around to see if a police car is following them, but she can't see anything. The rear window is blocked by an old picnic basket and by clothes from the metal wardrobe that Eva has stacked on the back seat. Underneath her, Ellen touches a lumpy plastic bag full of something that sounds and feels like coins.

Ellen sways as the car rumbles over the railroad tracks. Did anyone recognize her just now as she got in the car? She doesn't think so, although, if they did, what difference would it make? She would *like* to be caught and brought back. What does Eva think she's doing, anyway? Ellen gives her grandmother a sidelong glance as they drive onto Main

Avenue. Eva's hair, longer and grayer than Ellen realized, has come undone from a knot. She's muttering to herself and making unnecessary swerves, as if she sees traffic that isn't there. Eva drives up the bridge ramp.

"What's this all about?" Ellen asks, trying to mask her anger and impatience. "Do you have any idea what a mess you just caused?"

"I came for you," Eva says.

Ellen blinks. "You parked in the Ambulance Zone because you were looking for *me*? How did you know I was at the hospital in the first place?"

"You work."

"During the week, I told you. This is Sunday. I was only there by chance because my Grandpa's sick." Ellen sighs. "Where are we going?"

Heading down the bridge ramp, Eva doesn't answer. A car comes toward them and Eva veers over the solid white line.

"Watch out!" Ellen cries.

Eva, unruffled, recovers the wheel.

They are almost at Palmer Park now. Ben will be calling her house any minute, Ellen realizes. A little beyond the park is the turnoff for Bright Avenue. She could try to jump from the car, but Eva is driving awfully fast. Ellen looks longingly at her street as they fly by it.

Meanwhile Eva faces straight ahead. Without shifting gears, she turns sharply onto Tower Drive.

Suddenly Ellen knows where Eva is taking her. The road narrows to two lanes of blacktop. On both sides are dense woods, cool and ferny. She smells the fresh mint and pennyroyal that they used to gather. Sun filtering through the branches makes bright patches on the road. Birds warble. As the car noses upward, the picnic basket bounces on the back shelf. Eva, winding around the serpentine road, follows the white arrow marked WINDSOR TOWER.

"We're going to *Wunderlich,* aren't we?" Ellen asks.

Eva nods. Her expression softens.

Ellen remembers the note in red crayon that she once wrote to Eva. As recently as a few days ago, Ellen thinks, she would have loved the idea of this ride. Now that she's seen how things are, though, what can come of it except more disappointment for both of them? No more games! Ellen looks directly at Eva. "*Wunderlich*'s not there anymore, you know," she says.

Eva, with a smile on her face, drives on as though she hasn't heard.

"Grandma Eva—" Ellen's voice shakes. "The place has been torn down."

Eva's sneaker presses harder on the accelerator. "Down? No, *up.* Up the mountain!"

"There's no house there anymore," Ellen whispers. "Why are you bringing me up here? Please, let's go back."

120

"The end's come," Eva mutters, concentrating on the winding road ahead. "The end of the world." Her necklaces clink as she turns the wheel.

Ellen's voice is faint. "What makes you think so?"

"They've come."

"Who? Who's come?"

"The men."

"Which men?"

"Strangers with machines. Next they'll take things!" Eva murmurs. "The clothes, the money, her picture—up here they'll be safe."

"Grandma Eva—" Ellen stares through the windshield at the trees, which are sparser now. "Turn around, please. Take me home."

Eva's mouth twitches. "*This* is home."

"Please, let's go back," Ellen begs, her eyes moist.

"No, no. We can always come here, he says. We'll be safe."

Ellen slumps dejectedly on the cluttered front seat, and Eva, passing the turnoff to Windsor Tower, takes the private road that Ellen faintly remembers.

Eva is smiling now. "See?" she says, pointing to the bag of coins on the seat. "All we need."

The waitresses' tips, Ellen thinks.

Now they come to a dirt road that looks as if it's been recently widened. Eva, with a puzzled expression on her face, continues over bumps and ruts past a bulldozer and a pile of felled trees until she comes to a sign: TOWER LUXURY CONDOMINIUMS COMING SOON.

Eva slows down, looks ahead and behind her, and then creeps upward until they arrive at the remnant of the stone archway that once marked the entrance to *Wunderlich*. Eva stops the car and gets out.

Ellen, watching from the front seat, sees her walk to a nearby pile of stones—stones that were once part of *Wunderlich*.

Eva picks up one, then another. She looks at them, holds them close to her for a moment, and then lets them fall to the ground.

Ellen gets out of the car and goes to her grandmother. The two of them stand side by side, gazing in silence at the huge piles of stones by the road. Picking up a small one, Ellen offers it to Eva. "Keep it," she says, "to remind you."

Eva drops the stone gently into her bag, and the expression on her face convinces Ellen that, for the moment at least, Eva understands that *Wunderlich* is gone.

"It's okay," Ellen says softly. "It wasn't ours anymore. East Windsor is your house. Let's go back."

"No, no!" Eva trembles. "It's the end!" Reaching into the pocket of her cape, she pulls out a crumpled piece of paper and thrusts it into Ellen's hands.

"What. . . ." Smoothing out the wrinkles, Ellen reads it.

WINDSOR HEALTH DEPARTMENT
Re: Correction of unsanitary and unsightly condition of premises at 1302 East Windsor Boulevard.
Name of Owner: Mrs. E. Dohrmann

Dear Owner:
You are hereby notified that owing to your failure to respond to previous warnings of violations of the Property Maintenance Code of Windsor, we have, in accordance with department policy, authorized persons in our employ to remove trash, litter, debris, obnoxious growths and weeds from your premises, the cost of which removal will be added to your property tax bill.

NOTE: *Further, owing to your failure to respond to warning notices of additional violations (unsafe structure, defective handrails and balconies, general building blight) a warrant has been obtained for the inspection of the interior of your premises on Monday, June 19. Your presence is requested during this inspection.*

James Herman
Sanitary Inspector

Ellen nods. "Now I understand. Men from the Health Department came to your house. What did they do, cut down the weeds? Did they try to come in?"

Eva's head bobs in agitation. Muttering wordlessly, she grabs the letter and crumples it again.

"You don't want them to come back," Ellen says, taking the letter from her.

Eva shakes her head vehemently.

Ellen stands in silence for a moment, anger and impatience transformed to pity. Looking into Eva's anguished eyes, Ellen notices distractedly that she and her grandmother are the same height. Or is Eva a tiny bit shorter? "No more putting off," Ellen says, more to herself than to Eva. "Something's got to be done. Let's go." And to her surprise Eva takes the hand Ellen offers.

"I'll stop them from disturbing your things," Ellen says as she leads Eva to the car. "I want you to drop me off on Bright Avenue and then go home and stay there, okay? I don't know how long it will take me—maybe until morning—but I'll come to East Windsor as soon as I can and tell you how I made out. Don't worry. The men won't bother you tomorrow. Do you understand what I'm saying?" she asks as they get into the car.

Eva nods.

"And do you trust me to do what I said?"

Eva pauses for a second, then holds up her gloved hand with the aquamarine on it.

Ellen smiles. "That's right. You trust me. Shutting the car door, she watches Eva turn the key in the ignition. "I have a ring of yours, too, you know," Ellen tells her. "Do you know the one I mean?"

124

The motor starts up. Eva's eyes glimmer. "Purple," she says.

"Yes. Do you remember how I got it?"

Eva touches her cape pocket.

Ellen nods. "I've thought, off and on, of returning it, but I haven't wanted to get either of us in trouble." She looks up. "And I've wanted to have something to remember you by. Shall we go home now?" she asks quietly.

Eva steps on the gas. The car rolls forward.

"My mother knows people at the Health Department," Ellen says as they bump along the dirt road. "Don't be upset about what they did today, Grandma Eva."

With a jolt the old car swings onto the hard asphalt surface.

Ellen braces herself against the dashboard. "No matter what happens from now on, I want you to trust me, okay? Trust me and remember that all I want to do is to make sure you're safe."

eighteen

"I'm at my house. I just got in."
Ellen, holding the phone tightly, sits in the kitchen
facing the front door.

"Where the hell've you been?" Ben's voice booms
through the receiver. "I called five or six times. Are
you all right?"

"I think so. Ben, listen, I have a lot to tell you
quick, before my mother comes back. She's at the
hospital visiting my grandfather."

"Hey, what—? Is it bad?"

"No, no. He's better, I think. I was there earlier.
When I left—you won't believe where I've been.
With Eva. She came to the hospital looking for me.
Caused this big uproar, parking in the space for the
ambulances."

126

"Oh, man. What then?"

"She took me up to *Wunderlich,* her father's old summer place near the Tower."

"What for?"

"She wanted us to stay there. She said it was the end of the world."

"Sure she doesn't know something we don't know?"

"Seriously, Ben, for a while there I was thinking, Please, just let me never see her again, that's all. My mother was right! And then, I don't know—I found these sad letters of hers and I saw her reaction up there on the mountain. Almost everything she ever cared about is gone, Ben. Every person. Even her housekeeper's dead, I found out. I can't just say '*So long.*'"

"What are you going to do?"

"Tell my mother, to begin with. I should have told her days ago."

"What can she do?"

"I'm not sure. Keep the Health Department from barging in on Eva tomorrow. At least that."

"Can I help?"

"You have to work tonight, don't you?"

"Yeah, by myself, in fact. Buddha called in sick."

"What's wrong with him?"

"I don't know. His uncle didn't tell me. Listen, can I do anything for you after work?"

"So late," Ellen pauses. "You know what would make me feel better? If you went by her house on your way home, just to see if . . . the cars are there and if things look the way they usually do."

"Sure. I'll check it out. Call me around midnight. And take it easy, okay?"

"I'm trying. Thanks a lot, Ben. I'll speak to you later."

"So long."

Ellen waits for the click and the dial tone. Then she punches out Josie's number, but before the first ring, she hears a sound on the stairs. She hangs up just as her mother opens the door of the apartment.

"Hi," Ellen says, sitting stiffly at the table.

"Hi there."

"What did the doctor say?" Ellen asks.

"He thinks Grandpa can come home tomorrow."

"That's great." Ellen folds her arms.

Her mother, in the doorway of the kitchen, smiles. "Everything all right with you?"

"Yeah. Yes. Did you—did you stop at Nonie's?"

"Not yet. She'd like us to go over there for supper. Is that all right with you?"

Ellen hesitates.

"Is it? I've hardly seen you in two days."

"I know."

"So we'll go then?"

She clears her throat. "Okay."

Her mother opens the refrigerator and takes out

a bottle of water. "I'm so dry. Would you like some?"

"No, thanks."

She pours and sips slowly. "Grandpa said you had a nice visit."

"Yeah. It was nice."

"You didn't stay long."

"The doctor came. I left when the doctor came."

"Well, I'm glad you got a little chance to—" Her mother looks at her. "You had a nice afternoon?"

Ellen nods.

"Good. Then we both missed the excitement over there. Eva turned Windsor General upside down this afternoon. Everybody was talking about it. She parked her car in the Emergency Zone and—"

Ellen lets out her breath. "I know. I'm the one who got her to move. I went away with her in her car."

Her mother's mouth twists awkwardly. "Oh, Ellen."

"And that's not all," Ellen says, meeting her mother's eyes. "She went there because she was looking for me." Ellen pauses. "I've seen her every day since my birthday. I spoke to her Thursday night in her car. I went to her house Friday and yesterday."

Her mother turns away.

"I said *I've been to her house,*" Ellen repeats.

Her mother faces her. "I heard you. *I heard!* Oh, Ellen!" She bites her lip. "After all we discussed!"

"We hardly discussed anything. You didn't listen to my side."

"Sides, sides! I thought we were on the *same* side!" Her mother's face collapses in pain. *"You approached her.* What for? Why didn't you tell me?"

"Because I knew you'd be mad!"

Her mother rocks back and forth. "Don't I have reason to be? It's the deception that hurts, the idea that I can't trust you." She stops to catch her breath. Her face is damp and red. "Josie egged you on in this, didn't she? She encouraged you to go up to Eva—"

"Don't blame Josie. *I* did it."

"Josie wasn't involved at all?"

"Only yesterday."

"So that's where you were when I was trying to let you know about Grandpa! Why is it that young people today are only attracted to whoever is odd? Anybody normal is too dull!"

"That's not true. I wish Eva wasn't odd. It can't ever be the same as it used to be!"

"That's exactly what I told you in the first place!"

"You were right. But what's going to happen to her? Alicia is dead—I saw the notice. The house is a pigpen. No electricity, no water. Eva's a wreck! Who's going to help her if we don't?"

Her mother's rigid body yields a little. "Alicia's

130

dead," she says. "Oh, no. Who looks after Eva then? Who cooks?"

"Nobody. She eats garbage."

Her mother winces. "Has she asked you for anything?"

"No. I took her food yesterday, but it was my own idea."

"That's all you've given her?"

Ellen, trying to recall, glances down at her hands.

Her mother is quick to notice. "Oh, Ellen, your new ring that Nonie and I—"

"I left it to show her I'd come back. Everybody else has deserted her, Mother! She'll die!"

"What about the lawyer? Where's the lawyer been all this time?"

"Some of the letters are probably from him. There's a mountain of mail there."

Her mother drops into the chair across the table from Ellen. "This is exactly what I wanted to avoid." She throws back her head. "Don't you see how—? Oh, Ellen, now what?"

"I thought maybe you could speak to somebody at the Health Department," Ellen says quickly. "They bothered her today and they're going back tomorrow. She's scared to death, Mother, and when she's scared she does dangerous things. I told her I'd come back. Maybe I should stay with her until—"

"Wait." Her mother grips the table firmly. "No

need for that. I'll call the Health Department social worker at home. I know her. Her office is near mine in the hospital."

"Can you get her to stop them from going there?"

Her mother lets go of the table. "That's not enough, Ellen. That's not enough."

"What else?" Ellen's voice cracks.

"Let's hear the social worker's opinion," her mother says softly. "You're right. We're involved whether we like it or not. We can't turn our backs anymore."

"I know. But what should we do? What will they do?"

Her mother's eyes snap shut. "Whatever we decide is best for everyone concerned." Opening her eyes, she looks directly at Ellen. "Meanwhile, there's something I'd like very much for you to do."

"What?"

"Stay over at Nonie's tonight. Sleep there. She's feeling very lonely. She'd be pleased if she thought it was your own idea to spend the night. Let's pretend it was."

"I told Eva—" She stops. "Okay, yes. I'll go to Nonie's. Can I talk to the social worker?"

Her mother is already flipping through the phone book. "Yes. I want you to. I'll make an appointment for both of us for the first minute she can see us."

nineteen

Nonie, glass in hand, passes by the television set. "Are you watching this, Ellen, or should I turn it off?"

"No. Go ahead. Turn it off." Ellen stretches restlessly in Grandpa's armchair.

"Nothing but trash on TV tonight. I'm so glad you're staying over." Nonie flicks off the television. "Are you sure you wouldn't like something to drink—some ginger ale?"

"No, thanks."

Nonie seats herself at the desk. "Look at me, drinking a glass of wine before I go to bed! My neighbor said, 'Try it, if you want to fall asleep.'" She sips cautiously. "It's hard, you know, falling asleep with so many things on your mind."

"I know," Ellen says. "Maybe I'd better have some, too."

"Do you mean it? I don't think a little would hurt you. It's nice and sweet—"

"Just kidding. I don't want anything." Sinking deeper into the chair, Ellen smells the familiar cooking odors and sees the slipcovers and dark polished wood that she knows as well as she knows her own living room.

"You don't have trouble sleeping, do you, Ellen? When I was your age, I slept like the dead." Nonie sets the wineglass on the desk blotter. "See this mess I got myself into here? I was going through these pictures to get rid of some of them." She picks up a handful of photographs. "Trouble is, once I start looking, I can't throw anything away. This dear little thing—know who she is?"

Ellen reaches for the photo. "Me in first grade." She hands it back.

"How about this one?" Nonie asks.

"Yeah. That one's funny."

"Oh, my word, where did this one come from?" Nonie's hand flies out so that she almost tips her glass of wine. "I haven't come across this in years. The Bachelors' Ball! Oh, my heavens!"

Ellen glances politely at the photograph.

"That was my one night in Windsor society." Nonie beams. "The year before I met Grandpa."

She pauses. "You know who *this* is, don't you?" she asks in an undertone.

"Who?"

She nods as Ellen recognizes the face. "Can you believe that's the same woman we saw in Zimmer's the other night?" Nonie studies the picture. "I'll never understand it as long as I live. She was the loveliest girl at that dance. We went to her house afterward. I hardly knew her at all, but she asked the whole crowd over. The only time I was ever invited there, including after your mother married Fred."

Ellen looks at the young Nonie, grinning as she links arms with her date, and at Eva, the most beautiful one in the picture. "What was she like then?"

"Oh, sweet and fluttery like a bird with fellows and girls her own age, but so meek with her father! One word from him and she'd jump. Well, she was all old Frederick had, you know, after his wife ran off."

"Why did she leave?"

Nonie's eyebrows arch. "For another man, they said. A musician, who convinced her she could have a career. The talk was that old Frederick was so shamed he never let Eva's mother's name be mentioned in that house again."

"It must have been horrible for Eva."

"Well, I guess so," Nonie says. "I'll never forget

something she told me privately the night I was there. She said she knew where her mother was, and she was going off to see her. Next thing we knew, though, she was married to Miles Dohrmann, a wealthy friend of her father."

"Was he nice?"

"Who knows? The one time I saw him was when your mother married Fred. Miles and Eva only lived together a short time, you know," Nonie says confidentially. "The rumor was that Eva's father arranged the marriage to keep Eva in money and out of trouble."

"You mean she didn't love Miles?"

"I never asked her," Nonie says. "I'm only repeating the rumor."

Ellen hesitates. "Did you mind when Mom married into Eva's family?"

Nonie picks up her wineglass. "It's water under the bridge, Ellen. Young people do what they want."

"What was Eva like at the wedding?"

"Oh, still an impressive woman. The fur cape was new, I recall—a gift from her father." Nonie sips her wine. "He died soon after that. That's when she really went off the deep end. So sad. That pretty girl gone *off*, like a piano out of tune. Do you know what she had the nerve to ask us once? She asked if you could live with her, up there on the mountain. Can you imagine?" Nonie puts down her glass with a *clunk*. "Oh, my," she says, pressing her hands to her temples. "I believe that wine's made me dizzy. I should go right to bed."

"Here, I'll help you." Ellen offers her arm.

Nonie leans on her. "I don't think we're going to have to worry about Eva much longer."

Ellen looks at her. "What do you mean?"

"I hear she's failing fast. Not that I wish her ill. I don't wish anybody ill."

They walk in silence to the top of the stairs. Nonie, dropping Ellen's hand, stands in the dark hall and seems reluctant to go to her room. "It's hard for me, Ellen, when Grandpa's not here."

Ellen nods.

Her voice wavers. "What'll I do, dear, when I'm alone?"

Ellen clears her throat. "Grandpa's probably going to come home tomorrow. And Mom and I are here if you need us."

"You know what I think sometimes?" Nonie says.

Ellen can't see her expression in the dark.

"I look at Eva Dohrmann, and I think, *That could be me!*" She laughs in embarrassment. "Oh, not quite so bad, you know—but that *could* be me, if I didn't have my family around me. Thanks for offering to stay over, Ellen. I miss our times together, don't you?"

"Yes."

Nonie moves toward her room. "You sleep well now, you hear? I'll make you a big breakfast in the morning."

"No, thanks," Ellen says. "Why don't you sleep late? I'm meeting Mom for breakfast."

"Oh, well, if she said so. Come back to us soon. This was so nice. Sleep tight now."

"Good night, Nonie."

Ellen waits until she hears the sound of water running before she goes downstairs to use the phone. It's almost midnight. She dials.

"Hi."

"Ben—hi. I'm at my grandparents'. You passed by Eva's?"

"Yeah. Everything's quiet. All three cars were there. What's happening with you?"

"I told my mother. She was furious at first, but she came around. She called the Health Department social worker, and we're seeing her first thing tomorrow. I don't know when I'll get to Eva's."

"You sound sort of down."

"Yeah."

"How come?" Ben asks.

"Because it's the end."

"The end of the world?"

"The end of hers, probably."

"You did everything you could. Listen, I'll check out her place again in the morning. When you get out of that meeting, call me at home."

"Good. Thanks a lot." Ellen is silent for a second. "When this is over, maybe we'll see each other."

"I'm counting on it. Hey. On the lighter side.

Guess why Buddha called in sick. Because he's got an ear infection."

"From the pool?"

"No, from piercing his own ear! Sad, huh? Talk to you tomorrow."

"Okay. Good night, Ben."

twenty

"Hi, Ellen, good to meet you. I'm Marcia Ornstein. I'm the social worker. I know your mother—"

"Hi." Ellen looks at the conference table set up with coffee cups and a file folder.

Marcia takes off her dark-framed glasses. "I'm really glad your mother called. The timing is fantastic. I've been arranging this conference for a week, but we didn't expect to have any relatives here. The others will join us in a few minutes."

"My mother's on her way," Ellen tells her. "She had to speak to my grandfather's doctor."

Marcia pulls out two chairs. "Here, let's sit down."

Ellen, taking the chair that's offered to her,

glances around the conference room with its bare beige walls. After two summers as a candystriper, it's just dawning on her now—she can't stand hospitals.

Marcia pushes her hair behind her ears. "So. I understand you're the only one who's been directly in touch with your grandmother."

"Yes."

"We've been trying to figure out the best way to approach her for a while now," Marcia says. "First the Sanitary Inspector started getting complaints from Mrs. Dohrmann's neighbors. Then the fire department contacted us. Now we've got a whole folder—" Marcia, sitting back, looks at Ellen. "You're very worried about her, aren't you?"

"Yes."

"Well, first of all, don't worry about the inspection. Nobody's going to just pop over there, okay?" She flips through the folder. "The more I find out about this situation, the more surprised I am that no crisis has come up until now. I saw your grandmother the first day I came to Windsor. Two years ago—in the Square. I'm from New York, and I remember thinking how in the Port Authority Bus Terminal or in Greenwich Village nobody would look at her twice, but here—"

"Maybe she should have gone there to live," Ellen says. "She used to talk about taking me to New York."

"I don't happen to think she'd have been better

off in a big city. I admit though, that it's tricky handling her problems here. Because your grand-mother has an income, and because her family—your father's family—was well known, nobody's wanted to interfere. It's finally coming together, though." Marcia holds up a letter. "This floated around from one department to another for weeks until it landed on my desk. It's from her lawyer, Arthur Hintz, a partner of the Philadelphia firm that's been managing your grandmother's trust for years. He says he's been trying to get in touch with her—"

"There are lots of unopened letters at her house," Ellen says.

Marcia looks at the clock. "We're waiting for Mr. Hintz now. And Dr. Ferrara."

"He's from . . . the sixth floor?"

"Yes, he's the Director of Psychiatric Services. It's routine to ask him to sit in on a conference like this."

"He knows who my grandmother is?"

"He's read the file. Maybe you'll be able to tell him a little bit more about her. He works with older people a lot."

"He won't want to meet her, will he?" Ellen asks. "She's really scared of strangers."

Marcia looks at her intently. "You feel responsi-ble for her, don't you?"

"There's nobody else."

Marcia leans forward. "What we're going to try to

142

do is to find a way to share the responsibility, Ellen, so everything doesn't rest on your shoulders. You were close to her when you were little, weren't you?"

"Yes."

"I was too, to my grandmother. It was very hard for me when she died. But this is harder, isn't it?"

Ellen nods.

"I think I know what you're feeling," Marcia says. "Where there's life, there ought to be hope, but you're afraid to hope—"

Voices sound in the hall.

"Excuse me, Ellen. Come in!" Marcia gets up. "Mr. Hintz? And—oh, good. Everybody's here."

"Arthur Hintz."

Ellen watches him put down a slim briefcase and extend his hand.

"Nice to meet you. I'm Marcia Ornstein. Mr. Hintz, this is Ellen Dohrmann and her mother, Dorothy. How's your father, Dorothy?"

"Better, thanks."

"That's good. And this is Dr. Tom Ferrara, everybody—Director of Psychiatric Services."

Dr. Ferrara eases into the chair across the table from Ellen. "Good to meet all of you."

Ellen sizes him up. Young looking. Soft mustache that's the same light brown as his hair. Summer sports jacket. No little white coat!

"Please sit down—Dorothy, Mr. Hintz. How about some coffee?"

"Fine." Dr. Ferrara, sliding his chair back, reaches for the pot and pours.

As her mother sits down next to her, Ellen whispers, "Grandpa's going home?" Her mother nods.

Mr. Hintz sits at the far end of the table, and Ellen takes a steaming cup from Dr. Ferrara. Putting on her glasses, Marcia says, "I think everybody here is familiar with the facts. What we're dealing with is a seventy-year-old woman whose competency is doubtful, who probably shouldn't be living alone, but who isn't willing to cooperate with the available agencies. In personal terms," Marcia says, looking up, "we have a long-time, well-known resident of Windsor, grandmother of Ellen, who's at a point where she can't be trusted on her own, yet she still has a strong urge to be independent."

Marcia turns over a paper. "I have letters and memos from various agencies, plus the tax collector, the utilities, and Mr. Hintz's firm, all raising questions about Mrs. Eva Dohrmann's situation. Everybody wants to do the right thing for her. I've spoken to each of you separately, but now it's time to see what we can come up with together. As you know, Ellen is the only one who's had any personal contact with Mrs. Dohrmann, so first I'd like to know if she thinks there's any chance of these problems being solved by hiring a live-in housekeeper or a homemaker who would go in for a few hours a day."

144

"She's afraid of strangers," Ellen says. "She won't speak to anyone but me. Sometimes she won't even speak to me."

"From what I gather, she's gotten very hostile to strangers," Ellen's mother says. "I don't think you could find anyone willing to work for her."

Marcia, removing her glasses, rubs one eye gently. "Ellen, do you see your grandmother living alone in her own home anymore—as far as safety is concerned?"

"No, but—what would happen to her?"

Mr. Hintz peers over his briefcase. "An institution—"

Ellen shakes her head. "Not Crocker State!"

"That's not the only alternative," Dr. Ferrara says. "This hospital right here serves short-term patients. If we're talking about long-term care, there are private hospitals, homes, boarding houses, halfway houses, clubs—"

"I don't think my grandmother would go to any of those places. Unless you dragged her."

Dr. Ferrara smiles. "Let's hope it won't come to that. I'd like to ask Mr. Hintz about Mrs. Dohrmann's financial situation. That may help us see what the alternatives are."

Mr. Hintz opens his briefcase. "I don't think you'll be surprised to hear that there have been some problems in administering the trust for Mrs. Dohrmann, set up by her late husband Miles over forty years ago."

"Her husband?" Ellen's mother says. "I thought it was her father's money."

"No, her husband set up a trust back in 1936, at the time they began living apart. It provided for both Mrs. Dohrmann and her father, Frederick Ehrhardt, who I believe lost most of what he had in the Depression. The hitch is that this trust has been active so long that I'm the fourth attorney to manage it. If I had been involved longer, or if I lived in Windsor, I'd have known long before this about Mrs. Dohrmann's—lifestyle. Until today I had never seen the house."

"You saw it today?" Ellen asks.

"Yes. Well, I *tried* to see it this morning. I'm afraid Mrs. Dohrmann didn't want to see *me*. At any rate, my firm has mailed quarterly checks for over forty years to Mrs. Dohrmann with no complications until about two years ago."

"That must have been when her housekeeper left," Ellen's mother says. "Alicia Donovan."

"Yes," Marcia says. "Up until then Mrs. Dohrmann seems to have been able to get by, even with all her eccentricities. As I see it now, the main question is this: If she can't continue to live by herself, what else is open to her? Can you give us some idea of what she can afford, Mr. Hintz?"

"With the sale of the house, the income ought to be enough to maintain her in a private institution." He looks from one of them to the other. "The way it sounds, though, there may be some difficulty in

146

getting her to go voluntarily. If she won't go on her own, is anybody here prepared to go through the process of committing her?"

Ellen coughs.

Her mother rests a hand on the back of Ellen's chair.

The room is silent.

"Dorothy," Marcia asks, "where would you like to see your mother-in-law go?"

"Into a private hospital, of course—a good one—if we can get her to go."

"And if she can't be persuaded to go voluntarily?" Marcia asks.

Ellen's mother's hand slips off the chair. "Then I'm prepared to find two doctors to declare her incompetent. I know that might limit us to public institutions—"

Ellen whirls around. "Crocker State?"

"Wait a minute," Dr. Ferrara says. "I don't think anybody here is eager to send *anybody* to Crocker State." He turns to Ellen. "Don't you think we ought to give your grandmother a chance to admit herself?"

"She'll hate *any* hospital," Ellen says.

"What makes you so sure?" Dr. Ferrara asks.

"Because I know her."

Dr. Ferrara nods. "I agree. You do. Better than the rest of us. So if we want to avoid Crocker State, maybe you can help."

"How?"

"Help to convince your grandmother to try this hospital right here," Dr. Ferrara says. He pushes his chair back. "Would you like to see where I work, upstairs on the sixth floor? That would give you some idea of what we're talking about. I have an errand to take care of up there. How about coming with me and taking a look?"

"Right now?"

"Sure, if it's all right with your mother and everybody else. They'll probably still be tossing this around when we get back. What do you say?"

"Good," Marcia says.

Ellen's mother nods.

"Ellen? What do *you* say?" Dr. Ferrara brushes his mustache with his fingertips, and Ellen gets up slowly.

twenty-one

Dr. Ferrara presses the elevator button. "Well," he says, shoving his hands into his pockets, "from what you've been telling me, it sounds as if you handled yourself pretty well with her. It's been rough on you, hasn't it?"

"Yes."

"But your grandmother's never been violent."

"Not really. Two days ago, though, she locked my friend Josie in a wardrobe and went off in her car with the key."

"What did you do?"

"These friends of ours came by, luckily, and got Josie out."

"Your grandmother showed no concern?" Dr. Ferrara asks.

Ellen shakes her head. "I didn't even ask her afterward why she did it. I don't think she knows."

Dr. Ferrara pushes the button again and whistles while the arrow above the elevator descends. "I understand you're an old hand around this place," he says. "This is your second summer as a candy-striper?"

"Yes, and the last one, I hope." Ellen leans against the cool wall.

"You've had it with the world of medicine?"

"I hate hospitals."

"Don't let that get out. I wouldn't want an epidemic of that around here." He looks at her. "What bothers you about us? *Us.* See how I identify with this place?"

"I don't like the smell, and the whispers, and when I came here to my mother's office when I was little, I used to have bad dreams afterward."

"Why did you volunteer, then?"

"Because my mother arranged it."

"Do you always do what your mother wants you to do?"

"Almost always, until now. She didn't want me to see my grandmother."

"I know."

The elevator stops. Dr. Ferrara jingles coins in his pocket as the elevator rises. They get out on the sixth floor. "This will be a quickie tour," he says, "but if you have any questions, ask. We try not to be too institutional around here. No uniforms, see?

150

Nurses and patients wear their own clothes. Smell the pizza for lunch?" Dr. Ferrara opens the door to the Psychiatric Unit.

"It's not locked?"

"You can walk in, but you can't get out without a key. This is it. One floor of one wing—room for twenty-five people."

Ellen looks up and down the corridor. The walls are bright yellow. The bulletin boards are full of notices. Somebody is using the pay phone. A few people are standing around in the hall and in the doorways. It doesn't look much different from the college dormitory she once visited.

"Let me introduce you." Dr. Ferrara leads Ellen inside a windowed cubicle, where several staff members are examining charts at a table. "Stay right where you are, everybody. This is Ellen Dohrmann. She came to see what we do here all day. This is Helene Danzig and Tim O'Neill —they're nurses—and Barbara Kulp, our psychiatric social worker. We're going to have a look around. See you later."

Ellen follows him into the hall again.

"Hi, Dr. F.!" A black girl wearing glasses and a baseball hat calls to him.

"Hi, Ceil. You're looking good."

"So let me go home."

"Soon. We'll talk about it today. Ceil, this is Ellen."

Ceil smiles. "Hey. You just come in?"

151

Ellen hesitates.

"She's visiting," Dr. Ferrara says.

Ceil squints behind thick lenses. "Oh. Seeing how the other half lives, huh?"

Dr. Ferrara turns Ceil's hat around by the visor. "Yeah, the smart-aleck half."

Ceil backs off. "Not me, Dr. F.! No more, I swear. I'm not throwing water on nobody no more. Can I go home?"

"We'll discuss it. See you at three."

"Not if I see you first! So long, *visitor*."

Dr. Ferrara stops in the doorway of the kitchen with its huge coffee machine and circular table. "This is where patients get themselves a snack whenever they want one."

Ellen, watching as a young patient helps an older one drink from a cup, tries to picture Eva here. Eva would never accept help from strangers. Eva wouldn't stay in the first place. "Do the patients ever try to sneak out?" she asks in a low voice.

"Oh, sure," Dr. Ferrara says. "But not very often, and when they do try, we're almost always able to talk them out of it. They're here voluntarily, after all, so nobody's a prisoner. Hello, Betty," Dr. Ferrara calls. "Hello, Maria."

"Oh, oh, Doctor!" The older woman turns around in her chair. "I can't move my arms today, Doctor. My arms won't move."

"We're getting the X-rays this afternoon, Betty. I'll go over them with you."

152

"My arms are paralyzed, Doctor," Betty sobs. "What'll I do?"

"I'll examine you when you come in. How's the coffee?"

"I can't lift the cup. My arms won't move."

"Maria's helping you. Excuse me now, Betty."

"Good-bye, Doctor." Betty waves to him.

"She moved her arm," Ellen says as they go down the hall.

"Yes. We took X-rays, but we don't expect anything to show up. Betty's been a patient here four times. You could say that's discouraging, and yet each time she's improved enough to go home for a while."

Dr. Ferrara's crepe-soled shoes make a squishing sound as he and Ellen move on down the corridor. "This is Occupational Therapy," he says.

The bright room is full of activity and sound. A dozen or more patients are at work on various projects. Ellen watches an old man wrap wool around a spindle. An obese woman is weaving a mat. Two young women, their projects off to the side, are talking to each other a mile a minute. How would Eva act in this room? Ellen wonders. Maybe she would enjoy making paper flowers again after all these years. Or doll house furniture, like that girl at the end of the table. Or maybe Eva would just sit by herself in a corner, like the young man with dark eyebrows.

"How about this?" Dr. Ferrara points to a painting in the display case outside the Occupational Therapy room. "This fellow is really talented. That's him in there—the one sitting in the corner."

Ellen stands in silence for a moment, looking at the water-color landscape. "It's great," she says. "Did he do it from memory, or—can they ever go out?"

"Sure. There are group activities outdoors. He painted that out in the hospital rose garden, for instance. And patients can get passes to go home for the day or overnight."

Ellen glances down the yellow corridor. "Still. Isn't it the *same,* day after day?"

Dr. Ferrara sticks his hands in his pockets again. "So is going to work or to school, isn't it? To some extent. The point is, it's often a relief to know what's going to happen tomorrow. To a lot of patients it's a *relief* to have some structure in their lives at last. Somebody like your grandmother, for instance, might adapt quicker than you'd imagine. It must be a strain on her, wondering each day if she's going to find something to eat. Here she'd have it provided."

Ellen shakes her head. "I can't believe she'd like that."

"She probably wouldn't at first. Chances are she'd keep up her same old habits—she'd hoard food, sneak it back to her room. She'd try to keep everybody away from her belongings. She'd imagine they were trying to take them from her. But she'd slowly adapt. And the way she spends her time here might not be that different from her life on the outside, except that here the environment would be safe."

As they walk down the corridor past the bedrooms, Ellen looks out a window. "She'd die without her cars."

Dr. Ferrara's eyebrows shoot up. "From what you've told me, she's likely to survive a lot longer without them than with them."

"I admit she's a terrible driver," Ellen says, "but—"

"Wait a second." Dr. Ferrara stops outside a room where the blinds are drawn. "Excuse me."

Ellen follows him with her eyes. She should turn the other way, but her curiosity is aroused. A man, dressed only in his underwear, is in there lying on the floor. Dr. Ferrara comes to the door and calls a nurse. Ellen moves on down the hall, where a girl with long red hair is pacing back and forth, singing to herself. Ellen smiles at her, tries to make eye contact. But the girl's stare is vacant, like Eva's is sometimes. Sad enough, Ellen thinks, to see an older person so out of touch, but a girl her own age. . . . She feels relieved when Dr. Ferrara comes out of the darkened room and joins her.

"What can you do for them?" Ellen asks in a rush. "What could you do for my grandmother if she came here?"

"Evaluate her thoroughly, including a physical

exam, in case some physical problem is making her psychological problems worse." He pauses. "She'd receive medication that would probably make her less anxious."

"Would it turn her into a zombie?"

"Not if the dosage was right. We're careful about that here."

"What if she wouldn't take the medicine?"

"This state is pretty strict about protecting patients' rights," Dr. Ferrara says. "But we do everything we can to get them to take the right medication in the right amount for the right length of time. That's what we're here for."

"You mean medicine could cure her?"

Motioning her on, Dr. Ferrara shakes his head. "No, it isn't likely to work a miracle. But medication isn't the whole story. If your grandmother were here, she'd have group and individual therapy daily. She'd be kept as busy as possible with activities. We'd be making long-range plans for an appropriate place for her when she leaves here."

"You'd be giving her *shock treatments*—" Ellen's voice breaks.

Dr. Ferrara stops walking. "Probably not. I can't say for sure, though, without knowing more about her. Come over here. Look in this room."

Ellen peers at a small contraption with wires attached. She glances at Dr. Ferrara.

"Not such a monstrous thing, is it? That machine is used for ECT, electroconvulsive therapy."

"Shock."

He nods. "It sounds barbaric to some people, but in my opinion shock treatments are badly misunderstood. I've seen excellent results in patients suffering from depression."

Ellen is only half listening. In her mind she's seeing Eva as she's seen her in the past week: hunched over the wastebasket behind Zimmer's; dripping strawberry juice down her neck as she eats; parked in the Emergency Zone. "How did she get like she is?" Ellen blurts out. "Why does she do crazy things?"

"I'd have to have a lot more information before I could answer that," Dr. Ferrara says, leading Ellen into a large sunlit room with couches and a piano. "In general, people who hoard have so much missing from their lives that they try to make up for it by holding on."

"She's missing a lot," Ellen says.

Dr. Ferrara gestures toward the couch. They sit down.

Ellen looks at him awkwardly. "There's something I've wondered about—" Her voice falters. "She's my *grandmother*. The same family. Is there any chance—"

"That you could end up like Eva?" Dr. Ferrara shakes his head. "The argument's been raging for years about which counts more, heredity or environment," he says. "Let's put it this way, if a family has a history of mental illness, then I would wish for them an environment that's especially wholesome, to compensate for the illness. First of all, in your family we're talking about *one case,* not a history of mental illness. And second, your environment seems to me to be excellent. Are you missing what Eva missed? Did your mother desert you when you were little?"

"No."

Dr. Ferrara smiles. "I have a strong feeling you're going to go through life with only the normal kinds of problems. What do you think?"

Ellen lets out her breath. "The normal problems are bad enough."

Nodding, Dr. Ferrara sits back on the couch. "Well, that was the tour. Let's see what I left out. There's a Ward Room down there, where we keep the patients' belongings that might be dangerous to them, like glass containers and razors. There's a Quiet Room, where a patient is put if he needs to be alone. We have a TV room. I'd show you, but I'm afraid I might get hooked on *General Hospital.*"

Ellen, smiling weakly, watches as an elderly woman comes into the room and wanders out again.

Dr. Ferrara is silent. He folds his arms. "What do you think?" he asks after a moment. "What do you think about getting your grandmother to come to this floor voluntarily?"

Ellen doesn't answer.

"In these days that you've been with her," Dr.

Ferrara continues, "how has she responded to things you've asked her to do?"

"I haven't asked her that much."

"You told me you asked if your girl friend could go with you to see her. And yesterday you asked your grandmother to come back from the mountain."

"Yes."

"Maybe, if the right chance comes up and if your mother approved, you could try asking Eva one more thing."

"She'd never agree to come here."

"Well, then there's nothing more I can say, I guess." Dr. Ferrara swings around on the couch. "The thing is, your mother and the rest of us feel she can't be left as she is. Eventually somebody's going to take action. If you were to influence your grandmother now, it would probably be much easier on her than leaving strangers to handle her later. Think about it," he says, starting to get up. "Talk it over with your mother. Think about how you might be able to get her here. We'll make it as easy for you as possible. Any time of day or night you can come to the Emergency Room. I'll alert the staff. If you come, they'll know where to reach me, and I'll meet you there as fast as I can."

"I can't believe she'd sign herself in."

"Look," he says, "you'll do all you can, that's all. We want to take the pressure *off* you, not put more on. Remember what I said. If you keep on having contact with her, and the opportunity arises or there's a crisis, and you want to bring her in, we'll be ready to go from there."

"Okay."

"You can call me anytime, by the way, to discuss anything. I've already told your mother that. I wish there was more I could do." He gets up. "Shall we see how it's going downstairs?"

"I told this friend I'd call him," Ellen says. "I'll be down in a minute."

"There's a phone by the desk. Do you have change?"

"Yeah, thanks." Her arms drop awkwardly to her sides. "And thank you for showing me. It's not what I expected."

"I had a feeling you ought to come up," Dr. Ferrara says. "Okay, then. I'm heading back to the meeting. Ask Helene to let you out when you're ready. See you in a few minutes."

"Thanks again," Ellen says as Dr. Ferrara unlocks the door and lets himself out. Then she goes to the phone and drops a coin in the slot. While she's dialing, her eyes stray to a printed form tacked to the bulletin board.

> *I, _____, desire to be accepted as a voluntary patient for care and treatment in Windsor General Hospital and agree to abide by all the Hospital Rules and Regulations . . .*

The phone rings.

"Ellen." Ben's voice is like a command.

"Yes. What? What's happening?"

"Can you come right over to Eva's?"

"Why? What's wrong?"

"I just came running back, hoping you'd call. I thought I saw smoke there."

"Did you call the fire department?"

"Not yet. I'm not positive it was smoke. Plus, don't worry—she isn't there. One of the cars is gone. I'm going right back. Can you meet me? How can you get here fast?"

"Cab," she says. "I have money. I'll leave right now. See you."

twenty-two

"This one, right here," Ellen says. The money is counted out in her hand.

"Thanks." The cab driver makes a move to open the door for her, but she gets out quickly by herself, a few houses before Eva's. She hesitates until the cab has gone and then half runs uphill.

She can see the red tile roof. If there's smoke, it's not visible yet. The peaceful sameness of the boulevard reassures her a little as she passes the Riegels' garden. By the time she gets to the edge of Eva's property, the effects of the Health Department's cleanup campaign are obvious. The prairie of tall grass is short and mangy now, like the fur on Eva's cape. Without the heavy cover of weeds, the house looks even more sad and bare than before.

Coming through the gateposts, Ellen spots the two cars with flat tires. The third is still missing. Maybe Eva is annoyed that she's taken so long to come back. Or Eva's been scared off by the sight of Mr. Hintz. Ellen checks carefully, but there's still no sign of smoke. "Ben?" she calls. He's probably decided to go inside. She hurries across the stubble of grass to the porch.

The remnants of Saturday's lunch are still there, exactly as they left them. One thing strikes her as unusual though. The French doors are closed tight. Ellen pulls. Odd. They seem to be stuck. Shielding her eyes, she tries to peer into the living room, but something is in the way. It takes her a few seconds to figure it out. A wooden plank has been nailed across the two doors on the inside. "Ben!" she calls again. What is this? And then the explanation hits her. The Health Department has come again. They've gotten their wires crossed. While Marcia's meeting is still going on, the inspector has come and condemned the house.

"Ben?" She shakes the doorknobs in frustration. When did the inspector come, while Eva was still at home? No wonder she took off! Ellen pounds on the door for a few seconds, and then, stopping to listen, she thinks she hears the sound of hammering inside the house. Somebody from the department must still be in there. She's got to get in, to find out who it is and what's become of Eva.

Her head isn't very clear, but she goes over in her

mind the various entrances to the house. Certain ones are blocked with furniture, she recalls. Others are locked with chains. She looks up hopelessly at the second-story windows. And then she thinks of the summer kitchen and of Toby the sheepdog's door.

Ellen runs down the steps and around to the back, where bits of mown grass catch in her sandals. She stops by the side of the summer kitchen. Toby's swinging door is off its hinges, on the ground. The opening looks narrower than she remembers, but, as if she were a kid again, she drops down and thrusts her head through the hole. Years ago she could chase Toby through here with room to spare. Now she hunches her shoulders and wriggles. Her blouse creeps up. Her stomach scrapes the gritty floor, and a familiar musty odor comes back to her. In the corner she can see the dollhouse draped in a white sheet. If her shoulders go through—and they do—then she'll make it. Her hips offer resistance, but she gives a final twist and gets to her feet.

Without taking time to look at the dollhouse, she goes to the place where she remembers there used to be a door. She pushes and it opens, just as it always did, into the dark storage place that ought to lead to the living room. Groping along, Ellen can still hear the tap-tapping sound somewhere over her head. What a farce—Marcia's telling her 'No one's just going to pop over there.' Ellen stumbles, catches her balance. Where the light is coming through a crack, that's the place to try. She pushes again. A door opens and she's in Eva's living room.

Ellen sniffs. The smell is strong, even if the smoke is only a trace. The fireplace has been used. She comes closer. They've used it to burn some of Eva's junk!

Standing by the hearth, she can't believe the stupid way they've gone about it. A few things lie between the andirons—a dress, a picture frame, the statue of Schubert, some letters—but they're only scorched, as if the sanitation people were in such a hurry they didn't bother to open the flue or to use kindling. Matches are strewn all over.

Ellen lifts the statue out of the rubble, brushes it off, and searches for a place to put it. On the wicker table? Not enough room. She walks over to the desk. *What a mess.* Has the cleanup committee been rummaging here, too? Setting down the statue, she notices a brittle sheet of paper spread out on the desk top, as if someone has just been reading it. What nerve, strangers prying into Eva's mail! Ellen sees the date 1930 in spidery handwriting. The signature is Eva's father's. Her eyes run down the page.

I have considered sparing you the news of these setbacks, but decided you must be prepared for the worst if it comes. The worst possible thing, of course, would be losing the East Windsor house.

We could go up to Wunderlich to live permanent-
ly, but I can't help feeling it would be <u>the end of</u>
<u>the world</u> if East Windsor were taken from us. Do
you know, Eva dear, I sometimes think I would
rather see the place go up in smoke than have it
fall into the hands of strangers!

Ellen reads through the rest of the letter quickly, then returns to the lines about the East Windsor house. Her eyes move from the faded stationery to the pathetic, blackened objects in the fireplace. The hammering upstairs starts in again. Shoving the letter into her pocket, she crosses the junk-lined path to the stairs and climbs as fast as she can. *I sometimes think I would rather see the place go up in smoke* . . . The sanitary inspector hasn't been here after all. By the time Ellen gets to the top of the steps she's sure of that, and her belief is confirmed by the sight she sees through the open door of the music room. On the floor, in the middle of the oriental rug, is a scattering of matches and a pile of papers that seem to be curled up at the edges. At the window, hammer in hand, is Eva, trying to nail the window shut.

For a few seconds Ellen watches as Eva lays down the hammer and reaches for a large silver cigarette lighter on a nearby table.

"Don't!" Ellen cries.

Eva, turning around, faces her.

Ellen clears her throat. "I'm sorry it's taken me so

166

long to come back. I've been trying my best. Please don't use that."

Eva looks first at the lighter, then at Ellen. "How did you get in?"

"I squeezed through Toby's door."

"It's the end," she says, her body heaving. "Today is the end." Her dazed expression suddenly changes to concern. "Go, go!"

"Why?"

"Before they come back." Eva tries to steer her clumsily to the door.

"Who? Mr. Hintz, the lawyer? He won't be back."

"No, no—police!"

"Wait." Ellen refuses to budge. "I don't believe you. The police aren't coming here. Nobody wants to bother you or take anything away from you, I swear. Everybody's trying to help."

Eva shakes her head. "Go, go! Police—they want it."

Ellen stands firm. "Want what?"

"The ring," Eva whispers. "The purple ring."

Ellen looks at her skeptically. "How did they find out I have it?"

"Go!" Eva insists.

Ellen shakes her head. "I think you want me out of here so you can try to burn the house down. I read that letter from your father, Grandma Eva. I don't know if you're burning things because of that or not, but if you are, you must stop. When he said it would be the end of the world if you lost East

Windsor, he didn't mean for you to set fire to the house. If you ask me, it was a dumb thing for him to write."

Eva's mouth twitches violently.

"It seems to me that if he loved you," Ellen says, "he'd want you to be safe, like I do."

"Safe, yes. Go!"

"Not unless you come with me."

Eva shakes her head. "No, no, my things!"

"We'll take as much with us as we can," Ellen says in a rush. "We'll go in your car. Wait—where *is* your car—the one you've been driving?"

Eva's eyes are glazed over in confusion.

"Never mind, we'll leave without a car."

"You. *You* go."

"I'm not leaving this house without you." Ellen, coming closer, notices now for the first time that one of Eva's gloves is torn and scorched. "What happened?" she asks.

Eva draws back.

"You burnt your glove, didn't you? You burnt your hand. Please let me see."

"Nothing!"

"If it's nothing, you shouldn't mind showing me," Ellen says, grabbing Eva's elbow gently but firmly.

Eva looks down, as if she hasn't been aware until this moment of her red and oozing fingertips protruding through the blackened leather. She bends one finger and winces in pain.

"You did burn it, didn't you? Let's take off your

glove." Eva's rings, she sees, are going to make it hard. Ellen pulls at the cuff, but the glove is stuck fast to the skin.

Eva lets out a cry.

"I don't think I can do it," Ellen says, fighting a wave of nausea. She holds Eva's arm protectively away from the cape. "It hurts a lot, doesn't it? You must come with me, Grandma Eva. With your hand like that you'll need help. You can't stay here. Come with me."

Eva backs away stubbornly and then stops, aware at the same time as Ellen of the crunching of pebbles and the screech of brakes outside. They both go to the window. Eva lets out another cry at the sight of the black patrol car that has pulled into the driveway behind the two useless maroon cars. Meanwhile, out on the boulevard a tow truck, pulling Eva's third car, has just arrived. And behind that is the fire chief's white sedan.

Eva grabs her canvas bag from the big leather chair and slings it over her good arm.

Ellen watches long enough to see an officer step out of the patrol car. Then she follows Eva. "You'll come with me now?" she asks.

Eva's eyes dart fearfully from the hallway to the bag on her arm.

"They'll come up here," Ellen says. "They will. They know how to break into houses. Come on." She shifts Eva's bag to her own wrist. "We won't let them find us. Come."

Eva insists on stopping to lock the music room door behind them. Then the two of them head downstairs.

"This way," Ellen says at the bottom of the staircase. She can hear voices now outside the French doors that Eva nailed shut. Holding Eva's good hand in hers, Ellen takes her through the dark storage passage. "Be careful," she warns her.

The door at the opposite end is still open, so the way is lit, and in a moment they're in the kitchen. Ellen feels like groaning at the sight of the heavy chain on the door to the outside. But Eva matter-of-factly reaches under her cape and hoists up a key. She fumbles, one-handed, until Ellen takes the key from her and unlocks the chain.

"If they see us, don't be scared," Ellen tells her as they hurry out the door and into the woods. With one hand she pulls Eva along and with the other she cradles Eva's bag. "I won't let them take your things," she says.

"To *Wunderlich?*" Eva asks after they've passed the gazebo and the outhouse.

"No. *Wunderlich* was torn down."

"Where?" Eva asks. Her makeup is smeared with perspiration now. She's panting.

"Where?" Ellen smiles. "We used to talk about going to New York, didn't we?"

Eva stops suddenly. "The cars! My things!"

"If we go back, they'll see us," Ellen says patiently. "We have your bag, right? And your jewelry and your cape—"

Eva, taking stock, reluctantly continues. They trip over fallen branches. The woods are thick here, but soon they will thin out where the street cuts through. "Where?" Eva asks again, distractedly.

"On a bus ride," Ellen says. "We're going on a bus—to safety."

twenty-three

Ellen feels curiously calm as she sits beside Eva on the bus, even though the driver keeps glancing over his shoulder and passengers can't help staring at them.

Eva's hat is in her lap, and hanks of hair cling to her cape. She's muttering to herself every time she touches her burnt hand, and Ellen is afraid the people around them can smell Eva as well as see and hear her. Still, Eva isn't doing anything too outrageous—just looking out the window and reaching over, off and on, to make sure her bag is still between them.

Josie would love to see this, Ellen thinks—the two of them riding together out of East Windsor.

"How's your hand?" Ellen asks. "Does it hurt much?"

But Eva is too involved in the sights outside to answer.

The brakes hiss and the bus comes to a halt. Ellen watches as people get on. A woman and a little boy sit down in front of them, and the bus starts up again. The seat quivers as the little boy settles himself.

Eva turns to Ellen. "Where?" she asks again.

"Away. To safety."

Suddenly the little boy is on his knees, facing them over the top of his seat. He stares at Eva, his tongue working furiously in his mouth. Then he thumps his mother on the arm. "Mom, why does that lady look like that?"

The mother yanks him down so that he disappears from sight.

"Ow!"

The bus driver is glancing over his shoulder.

The mother whispers.

"Why *not*?" the little boy asks.

"Where?" Eva repeats.

"Somewhere," Ellen says, and a fantasy plays before her eyes. No escape to a mountain this time. To a city, instead, throbbing with movement and sound, where every hour thousands of people that they've never seen before go by. And not one of them cares who they are, or how they look, or what they have in their bags and pockets.

173

The picture in her mind is so attractive that for the moment Ellen forgets to wonder how Grandpa is, and what happened to Ben, and what her mother is thinking in the conference room. She's so caught up in her fantasy that she remembers just in time to ring the buzzer.

The doors fly open. The bus shivers. Slinging the canvas bag over her arm again, Ellen helps Eva get up, while the little boy peers at them through the crack between the seats. Like marchers in a circus parade, they make their way down the aisle and onto the street.

Eva, holding her hand stiffly, looks up at the tall building in front of them.

She's confused, Ellen sees. The shock of leaving the house and the pain in her hand have put Eva into a kind of trance, so that she doesn't seem to know where she is.

Maybe she believes they're in New York. That's okay, Ellen thinks. Let Eva believe whatever she wants, as long as she comes with her willingly around the corner, past the Ambulance Zone and into the Emergency Room of Windsor General Hospital.

There's a lull inside the Emergency Room. No other patients are waiting. The nurse behind the desk looks disapprovingly at Eva. "Does she have medical insurance?"

"I don't think so. Can I take her in right away?"

"We have to see an insurance card."

"I'm Ellen Dohrmann," she says. "This is my grandmother. Please call Dr. Ferrara. He said I could come in at any time of the day or night."

"Dr. Ferrara? Oh!" The nurse disappears and another, friendlier-looking one takes her place.

"Ellen? Bring your grandmother right this way, please."

"Who's she?" Eva asks Ellen.

"It's okay. She's okay," Ellen assures her.

The nurse speaks to Ellen in an undertone. "We're calling Dr. Ferrara now. She burned her hand—is it serious?"

"I think so. I couldn't get the glove off."

"We'll take care of it immediately. Dr. Ferrara's on his way. Do you think you can get her to sit in that chair, behind the curtain?"

"I'll try."

"I'll be right outside if you need me."

Ellen pats the canvas bag protectively. "Let's see if your things are all right," she says, steering Eva to a chair beside the examining table. Eva's skin is dead white under the rouge. Her forehead is beaded with perspiration.

Like a mother trying to amuse a small child, Ellen reaches into the bag. "What's this?" She can hear them paging Dr. Ferrara over the P.A. "It's your makeup!" Ellen pulls out a can of lighter fluid. "And this? You don't need this anymore, do you?"

"Yes, yes, keep everything."

"Even this?" Ellen takes out an unwrapped cream-cheese sandwich from Saturday's lunch.

"Yes, yes."

Ellen holds up next a small picture in a frame. The brown-tinted photograph of a woman is old and worn under the glass.

Eva rears up. "Don't tell him. Don't tell!"

Ellen looks at the photograph. Eva's mother. It must be. There's a resemblance. "I won't tell. Don't worry." Ellen puts it carefully back in the bag and pulls out something else. "What are these?" she asks. The pack of dog-eared checks in her hand is bound with a rubber band. Flipping through them, she sees the wavy signature that she remembers from when she was little—*Eva Ehrhardt Dohrmann*. Eva's trust fund checks. Signed but not cashed.

"Give those to Alicia," Eva says.

"Okay." Ellen puts them in her pocket.

"Where are we now?" Eva asks.

Ellen pretends not to hear. *Hurry, Dr. Ferrara.*

Eva's lips twitch. "She played concerts in New York, you know."

Ellen nods. "Your mother, yes."

"Shhh!" Eva warns her.

"I won't tell anyone," Ellen whispers.

Outside, an ambulance wails. Eva, suddenly agitated, stands up and looks around. She pulls back the curtain.

Ellen inches closer to her.

The siren grows louder.

Eva shudders.

And before Ellen knows what's happening, Eva ducks under the curtain and hurries past the nurse.

Chasing after her, Ellen runs into the waiting room, where a man with a child in his arms has just gotten out of the ambulance. Behind him are two policemen.

Eva, when she sees them, gives a cry and slips into the corridor.

"Grandma Eva, they don't want *us*." Ellen, catching up with her, grabs a fistful of fur. She hangs on tightly.

Eva wriggles out of the cape and continues down the hall.

The cape hangs heavily in Ellen's hands for a moment. The friendly nurse, by her side now, picks it up when Ellen drops it and takes off after Eva.

Eva moves with surprising speed until she reaches the elevator, where she stops, disoriented and frightened by the people waiting there.

As they watch, Ellen rushes up and throws her arms around Eva. Eva struggles, but Ellen tightens her hold, shocked by how small and thin her grandmother is without the cape. "It's all right, it's all right," Ellen says over and over. But Eva keeps resisting, as the elevator doors open and a man with a soft brown mustache steps out and approaches them.

Ellen feels weak, but she does as she's told when Dr. Ferrara suggests that she keep hugging Eva. To her surprise, she doesn't pass out when she sees him push up the sleeve of her grandmother's dress and plunge in the needle. The sting causes Eva to twist violently. But then, giving up the fight, she lets herself be led back to the Emergency Room, where she sinks deeper into twilight as the sedative does its work.

"They had to cut the glove off," Dr. Ferrara says in a low voice to Ellen and her mother. He pulls the curtain shut between Eva and the woman in the other bed. "It's a second-degree burn, but there should be no problem getting back the full use of her hand." He nods toward Eva, who is stirring now, half sitting, half lying, beneath the sheets. "She's starting to wake up."

Ellen gazes at the white gauze bandage wound around Eva's right hand. They've cleaned Eva up in the Emergency Room. Her hair has been pinned back, perspiration and smudges have been wiped off her face, and her good hand has had the glove removed, too. "Is she going to be in a lot of pain?" Ellen asks.

"The nurse will give her something," Dr. Ferrara says. "She'll be pretty uncomfortable later, I imagine. She's going to be weak and sleepy for a while." Hands behind his back, he turns to Ellen and her mother. "I don't know how the two of you feel about this, but I'd like very much to be able to move her off the medical ward by tonight, up to the sixth floor."

Ellen's mother nods. "Yes, the sooner the better."

Dr. Ferrara takes a sheet of paper out of the inside pocket of his jacket. He pauses. "In that case, you know I need her signature on this voluntary admission form."

"How can she sign?" Ellen asks.

"Let's wait and see." Dr. Ferrara lays the paper on the table next to the bed. "When she's awake, if she can hold a pen, then—am I right that we all agree she should stay?" He looks at Ellen.

"Yes," Ellen says, "but how can she sign? She's right-handed."

"Maybe she can manage with her left. Her initials would be good enough. We've had patients admit themselves by signing an X."

"Without knowing what they were doing?" Ellen asks.

Dr. Ferrara's eyes meet hers. "I've had those same people say to me later, 'If you hadn't gotten me to sign in, I wouldn't be alive now.'"

"Isn't anyone sorry afterward?" Ellen asks.

"Then they can sign themselves out. That's the way it works here."

The voice on the P.A. begins its recitation of doctors. A steel cart clanks outside the door. Eva's eyelids bat open, then shut again. Ellen and her mother look at each other in silence.

"I'm sorry if I seem to be pressuring you," Dr. Ferrara says, "but if we don't get a signature she'll be released tomorrow or the next day. There won't be any medical reason to keep her longer. They need the bed."

Ellen's mother clears her throat. "She'd be on her own with her hand like that."

"We could order a home-care nurse," Dr. Ferrara says, "but that's no solution."

Ellen's mother, blinking behind her glasses, avoids Ellen's eyes. "I've made up my mind. If she can't sign, or won't, I'll begin the procedure to have her committed."

"That means Crocker or one of the other state institutions," Dr. Ferrara says.

Ellen looks away from both of them to Eva, who is suddenly awake.

Eva gazes in puzzlement at her bandage and at her bare left hand, and then, as if no one else is in the room, she stares at Ellen.

"I have your rings, Grandma Eva," Ellen says, reaching into her pocket. "See? Right here. The nurse gave them to me to keep for you." Jingling them lightly in her palm, she isn't sure whether the scowl on Eva's face is a sign of confusion or pain or anger. Eva's lips move but no words come out.

"Mrs. Dohrmann," Dr. Ferrara says gently, "we'd like to help you. We'd like you to stay here until you're feeling better."

Eva's scowl deepens. "Who is he?" she asks Ellen in a scratchy voice.

Ellen can feel the tension of her mother, standing behind her. "He works here," she says. "He's my friend."

"We'd like to have you stay here," Dr. Ferrara tries again, holding out the admission form now.

Eva shakes her head vehemently.

Ellen's mother leans forward. "You'll be fed. The food is fine here."

Eva glares at her. Ellen, breathing quickly, looks from one of them to the other. The hospital smell is getting to her, clouding her thinking so that she feels as woozy as Eva is. She bends over the pillow.

"Remember our bus ride, Grandma Eva?" Ellen forces a smile. "This is where I brought you—to safety." Eva's scowl is fading, at least. Dr. Ferrara, meanwhile, is fixing the admission form to a clipboard and taking out his pen. Ellen's mother rests her hand on Ellen's shoulder. The rings are digging into Ellen's palm.

"This is a good place, Grandma Eva," she goes on hesitantly. "I work here, and I know. It's nice, really. You can keep your own things with you. And get snacks whenever you want. There's a piano," she says brightly, hating the sound of her voice. She pauses. "Maybe you don't know what I'm talking about. Probably not. But please, please stay here?"

Ellen, taking the pen from Dr. Ferrara, curls the

fingers of Eva's left hand around it. Eva draws the pen up to her mouth, as if it's a lipstick.

Ellen's mother reaches out.

"No, Grandma Eva, it's a pen!" Ellen says. She concentrates on keeping her voice calm. "Remember when we used to make flowers at the kitchen table? And write things?"

Eva, staring at her bandaged hand again, fingers the pen awkwardly.

"You'd tear off big sheets of paper," Ellen rushes on, "and we'd fill them up with our initials." Ellen, without turning away, takes the clipboard from Dr. Ferrara and lays it gently in front of Eva so that her left hand just reaches it.

"Remember writing initials?" Ellen smiles. "E.E.D.—Ellen Elizabeth Dohrmann, and E.E.D.—Eva Ehrhardt Dohrmann." She could dash them off herself right now at the bottom of the clipboard, Ellen thinks, and who would argue? Her mother would be happy. Dr. Ferrara, too, probably. *The end justifies the means.* Ellen steers the pen in Eva's hand toward the blank space on the form.

Eva follows with her eyes.

"Can you do it with your left hand?" Ellen asks. "Can you write E.E.D.?"

Eva shakes her head.

Ellen hears a low moan from the bed on the other side of the curtain. Her mother turns around. Dr. Ferrara buzzes for a nurse. Ellen tunes out everything but Eva's dark eyes. "Come on," she

182

says playfully. "You remember! The dollhouse on the porch and sitting at the kitchen table—"

The pen falls out of Eva's hand.

Ellen pauses for a second. Then, taking one of the rings still clutched in her palm and slipping it on to Eva's finger, Ellen puts the pen in place again. "Please, Grandma Eva," she whispers, "write your initials here."

Eva raises her arm.

To see the ring better, Ellen thinks at first. But then to her surprise Eva scrawls two oversize, slanted E's on the sheet, somewhere in the vicinity of the dotted line.

"Good!" Ellen says. She can hear her mother behind her, nervously clearing her throat. Dr. Ferrara is smoothing his mustache. "Can you make a D?" Ellen asks.

And as if she recalls their old experiments with curlicues and fancy pen points, Eva, with a flourish, makes a D with a tail.

"Good!" Ellen says, her voice breaking. She quickly takes the pen and clipboard and hands them to Dr. Ferrara. ". . . so relieved," she can hear her mother whisper.

Meanwhile, Eva is looking at her questioningly.

"You handled it very well," Dr. Ferrara says.

Ellen, eyes stinging, shakes her head.

Dr. Ferrara nods insistently, but she looks away from him toward Eva, who is struggling to sit upright.

183

"Take it easy, Mrs. Dohrmann." Dr. Ferrara restrains her.

Fear comes over Eva's face. "My things!" She wrenches out of Dr. Ferrara's grasp.

"No, Grandma Eva, you'll hurt yourself!"

Dr. Ferrara holds Eva firmly by both shoulders, so that she gives up her attempt to get out of bed. Her face contorts as she bumps her hand. "My things—" she repeats pathetically.

And suddenly Ellen, listening to Dr. Ferrara's patient voice as he tries to calm Eva, can't bear this any longer—the smell, the sounds, the good intentions, the trickery. "I've got to get out of here," she says to no one in particular. Without any further explanation she heads for the door.

"Wait, Ellen—" her mother calls.

But she doesn't feel like waiting. So, ignoring her mother, she hurries from the room in the medical ward, down the elevator, and out the nearest exit.

twenty-four

Without a clear idea of where she's heading, Ellen comes out of the hospital and crosses Franklin Street. She moves on down the block until she can see the Square, where senior citizens are seated on benches on the brick island, and clusters of people are waiting for the bus. She should try to find out what happened to Ben, but she doesn't know where to call.

Drifting in the direction of the bus shelter, Ellen lets her imagination run wild again. From here to Philadelphia by bus—no, to New York. All by herself, with no messages left behind. Sleep at the Port Authority Terminal until she finds a job. . . .

"Ellen?"

She turns around.

Josie, barefoot and carrying her clogs, runs out of Giese's Grill and grabs her arm. "Oh, God," she shouts, "wasn't Saturday something else? It only hit me afterward. I wanted to call you yesterday, but I was so sick I couldn't make it to the phone." Josie studies her. "You too, huh? You look awful."

Ellen lets out her breath. "Not from Saturday. From what's happened since."

"*What*? Why didn't you call me? Have you seen Eva?"

"Yeah."

"What's wrong? Why are you looking like that? Like—*disaster*."

"Eva's in the hospital."

"Oh, no! What happened? *Hey*," Josie steers Ellen deftly around the potted petunias on the corner. "Let's sit, for God's sake. Here's a free bench. Now, tell me everything."

"Later." Ellen swallows dryly. "The whole story later. Yesterday—it's too much to go into. *Today*. Today I went to her house and found her with a burned hand, so I took her to the Emergency Room." She pauses. "This psychiatrist, Dr. Ferrara, wanted her to stay on his floor to be treated, but he couldn't put her there without her permission, so I got her to sign."

Josie's face falls. "She's in there for a while then."

Ellen nods. "Until they try medicine and place her somewhere else."

"No more East Windsor."

Ellen shakes her head. "It would take a miracle."

Josie's eyes flutter. "You must feel awful."

"Worse than awful." Ellen turns so that her face is hidden. "She didn't know what was going on, Josie! The police came, and her hand was hurting, and Ferrara gave her a shot—"

"What? Wait a minute." Josie takes her by both hands and pulls her around. "You're shaking, El. You're *shaking*. Come on, let's go and get you a Coke or tea or something."

"I don't want anything." Ellen looks at her and the tears spill over. "And don't tell me what I did was the only alternative! I know that, but it doesn't make me feel any better. I left her trying to get out of bed, calling for her things."

"Why'd you leave?"

Ellen sinks down on the bench. "Because I hate that place and *myself*, for tricking her!"

"How? What'd you do?"

"I pretended we were doing this thing we used to do—writing our initials. As if signing yourself into a mental ward was no bigger a deal than playing a game or a duet!"

"Maybe it isn't. Wait, don't get annoyed! Maybe it isn't for her, I mean. Maybe she'll be just as happy there—sneaking food to her room and all that."

Ellen looks at her. "That's what Dr. Ferrara said."

"So he ought to know." Josie jiggles Ellen's

187

hands. "Look at it this way, you can still visit her in the hospital."

"What makes you think she'll want to see the person who put her there?"

"Hey, what's this?" Josie squeezes. "What have you got in your hand?"

Ellen opens her fist. "Eva's rings. And my aquamarine. That's so weird. Look at the dents in my hand. I've been squeezing without knowing they're there."

"Come on, El, try to relax," Josie says, taking the rings from her and examining them with fascination. "So excellent! Take them to her. She'll appreciate some accessories. You know how blah those hospital gowns are."

"They wear regular clothes on the sixth floor."

"Cool. We can take her some. Hey, wait a second." Josie beats her own head with both fists. "Keep your big nose out of this, right? See, El? I learned my lesson. I'm keeping hands off from now on. She's *your* grandmother."

"I know." Ellen forces a smile.

"Here," Josie says, "put the rings in your pocket. They'll be safe until you get home. Then, know what you should do? Wrap 'em up fancy and give 'em to Eva like it's her birthday. Cheer her up. Cheer *yourself* up. Don't look at me like that. I know you're upset now, but in a couple of days you're going to see how much better she is, and you'll be glad it all happened like it did." Leaning down,

Josie puts on her clogs. "What do you say we do something—now, I mean—to take your mind off Eva's troubles? I'll skip work. We'll go to a movie or go swimming."

Ellen hesitates. "No, thanks. Thanks for trying, but I have to find Ben. He was supposed to meet me at Eva's and he didn't show up. I know, I know, I *told* you it was a long story! Eventually, I'll tell you everything, I promise."

"Swear?"

"Swear."

"Okay, then I'll let you go to Ben," Josie says. "He ought to be at work. I saw him pass by when I was eating at Giese's. When will I see you?"

"I don't know, but I'll call you as soon as I can."

Josie gives Ellen a hug. "Take it easy, okay? Wait and see. Eva's going to thank you when she's home again, all better."

Ellen starts to say something, then closes her mouth. Instead, she waves as she walks away from the bench and crosses the Square toward Zimmer's.

Ellen can hear Ben's voice over the clatter as she stands by the screen door of Zimmer's kitchen. She knocks.

"Hey!" Ben, dropping a pot, slips out the door and throws his arms around her. "You all right? I heard you were at the hospital."

She leans limply against him. "How did you hear?"

189

"The cops told me. You're okay? For sure?"

She nods. "The cops?"

"Yeah." Ben lets go of her. "Let me make sure Buddha's covering for me, so we can talk for a minute." He ducks into the kitchen. Then, coming out, he leads her to the edge of the porch, where they sit with their legs dangling.

"What a time! The cops thought I was trying to break into Eva's house," Ben says. "I was waiting for you, you know, when this patrol car pulls into the driveway."

"It's true then. Eva told me the police came."

"To see if she got home safe, that's all. They found her car a couple of blocks from her house— broken down. She must've walked home, but when I didn't see the car, I figured she was out."

"What did the cops do to you?"

"Took me to the station house. Asked me a thousand questions, like why I hang out at old ladies' houses. So while you were wondering where the hell I was, I was trying to convince the cops I'm a good guy. They finally brought me back to check out my story about the smoke."

"We were still there! You didn't hear us leave?"

"Nope. They made a lot of racket breaking in those side doors. Then they searched for her inside, until they got a radio call from the hospital that she was there—and you with her. She burned herself?"

"Yes, trying to set fire to the house."

190

"Man. Is she going to be okay?"

"Her hand, yes, but I don't know about the rest of her. She's in the psychiatric ward now. I tricked her into it."

Something crashes in the kitchen and Ellen cringes. "It was awful, Ben!" She sobs softly, her head on his shoulder. "She trusted me, and—"

"And you looked out for her, saved her life, maybe. It's rough, though. I see what you mean," he says, smoothing her hair. "Now what?" he asks quietly.

Ellen sits up. "I don't know."

"You'll go to see her?"

"If they let me. If she wants me to. If she doesn't hate me now."

"I doubt that." Ben takes her hand in his. "It's got to be tough, though, working in the same place where she is, wondering all the time how she's doing."

Ellen nods. "It's going to be so hard. If I had any nerve, I'd quit. I'd go away for the rest of the summer."

"Where to?"

"Anyplace. New York. The shore."

"What would be the attraction? Who do you know there?"

"Nobody."

Ben looks at her steadily. "Here you've got somebody."

"I know. I really appreciate everything you've

191

done. All of this would have been a thousand times worse without you. Still, I feel so *down*." Ellen blots her face with her sleeve. "I feel like changing my life."

"What do you mean? It *is* changed. All in one week you stood up to your mother, you saw your grandmother again, and you found this great, handsome intelligent guy, who—"

"I know, I know, Ben. I should be happy, I guess, but . . . I think I need to go home and be by myself until I hear how she is."

"Good idea. I'll drive you. Buddha's not too busy right now, and he owes me the loan of his car. Wait a second."

The screen door to the kitchen slams once, then again. Ben reappears, and Buddha, with a large gold ring in one ear, hangs out the door. "Watch yourself, Bernhauser! Nothing X-rated goes on in my car, you know. Not unless *I'm* there! Take it easy, Ellen!"

"You didn't tell him anything, did you?" she asks as they walk to the VW.

"Hell, no."

Ben starts up the motor and drives out of the lot in silence. Ellen looks straight ahead as the car chugs up the hill and over the railroad tracks. Her mind leaps from one thing to another. "Remind me to give you your bathing suit," she says.

"Keep it. To remember me by."

Ellen isn't sure why, but her eyes fill up again. "Thank you," she says.

Both of them are quiet for the rest of the ride.

Ben parks in front of her house. "Think you'll feel like talking some more later on?" he asks.

"Maybe."

"I get an hour off tonight from 6:30 to 7:30. How about meeting outside Zimmer's and taking a walk someplace?"

"I'll come if I can. Otherwise call me when you get off work, okay?" She opens the car door. "See you soon. And thanks again for everything, Ben."

She waves from the sidewalk. And then, as soon as the VW goes, she hurries upstairs to be alone in the dark, silent apartment.

Ellen lies on her bed, staring at the cover that Nonie made for her. *Grandpa*, she thinks suddenly. Did he get home all right? She'll call in a few minutes. First, though, there's something she's got to do.

Getting up, she drifts to the closet and lifts down the tin box with the purple ring in it. She carries it from its hiding place in her room to the kitchen, where, prying open the lid of the inside box, she takes out the ring and lays it on the table. It's been in the dark long enough. While she's sitting there, looking at the stone in its intricate setting, Ellen hears the downstairs door slam. Footsteps sound on the stairs. She feels herself tensing up, but she doesn't make any attempt to hide the ring.

The door to the apartment opens and her mother comes in. "I thought you might be here," she says. "I'm so glad you are."

Ellen, with her hands palms down on either side of the ring box, waits for her mother to notice it.

"I wanted to come after you when you left Eva's room," her mother says in a rush. "But Dr. Ferrara said, 'Give her a little time,' so I stayed there." She laughs nervously. "He's been right before, I hope he is again." She moves out of the shadows, closer to the table. "I'm glad I stayed, though. You'd have been pleased, too. A young nurse came in and acted just the right way with Eva, so that she calmed her down completely. I don't mean it's going to be a picnic—not for Eva or for the staff over there. But it's a good start. I left when they took her upstairs."

Ellen's mother takes a big breath. Ellen's eyes travel from her mother's face to the ring, and back again.

"I spent some time talking to Dr. Ferrara before I left the hospital, Ellen," she goes on eagerly, "and I think I understand some things better now than I did before. First of all, how hard this has hit you. Eva was something altogether different to you than to me. I have to keep remembering that."

"I'm sorry I ran out," Ellen says. "It was stupid."

Her mother's eyes meet hers. "Well, I'm glad I caught up with you. I've wanted to talk to you these last few days, but it's been so hard after all these

194

years of silence, and with Grandpa sick." She hesitates. "What I want to say is, I don't regret much in my life, Ellen. Certainly not marrying Daddy or coming back here to live. Or keeping my life separate from Eva's." She stops again. "The one and only thing I regret is not having been more open with you about Eva all along, not having talked it out more, to discover what you were feeling. I guess by making even the mention of her name off-limits, I put you in a position where you had to be deceptive, especially as you got older. I should have known you couldn't ignore her."

"I hated being sneaky."

"It must have been a burden—"

Palms sweating, Ellen sits up. Her mother has seen the box at last. Her eyes are on the ring inside it. Her bland face is animated now.

"You're keeping Eva's rings safe for her, I see. Are you going to take them with you tonight?"

"Tonight?" Ellen doesn't recognize her own voice.

"When you visit. Visiting hours are three times a week. Dr. Ferrara thought you might want to stop in after seven."

Ellen, feeling as dizzy as if she's just played Quarters, picks up the ring box and thrusts it at her mother. "This isn't one of those. I've had this ring for seven years. Look!" She points to the raised gold lettering.

"Main Avenue Jewelers. . . ."

Ellen, breathing shallowly, watches as her mother's curiosity turns to puzzlement and, finally, to slow comprehension.

Her mother sinks into the chair across from Ellen. "The missing ring," is all she says.

The words are spoken so low that Ellen can barely hear them. The disapproval, the anger she's feared all this time—where are they? "It's been in my closet since that day," Ellen tells her. "I wanted to let you know. I almost told you, lots of times. I took it from her so she wouldn't get caught with it. Afterward, I was afraid of what you'd say."

Her mother, touching the ring, blinks as if she's fighting back her own tears. "What a burden," she whispers. "How in the world did you bear it?"

twenty-five

The evening is hot, but Ellen and Ben don't notice as they sit on the bench in the rose garden. Goldfish poke at the surface of the pond. Maple trees form a canopy. If it weren't for Windsor General in the background, they could just as well be in the country.

Ben rests his arm on the back of the bench. "So it's okay with your mother?"

Ellen nods. "She suggested it. She said they can easily get a replacement for me at the hospital. They have a waiting list. She said she thought it would be good for me to do something else."

"Where is it you're going to be—Palmer Park?"

"Yeah. The playground staff is putting on a

197

musical in August. If I don't get a part, I'll do props."

Ben's arm slips off the bench and onto her shoulder. "Nervous?"

"A little."

"How did it go this afternoon, being by yourself?"

"I'm over the worst, I think."

"Your mother helped, right?"

"Yes. I should have told her about the ring ages ago. I should have told *you* before just now. Or Josie. Or anybody. It's such a relief!"

"What did your mother say about it?"

"We're going to the jeweler's tomorrow. We'll explain the whole thing and ask him how much it would cost to buy it, or to pay back the insurance company, or whatever."

"That's cool. Does she know how Eva's doing?"

"She was doing all right when my mother left." Ellen lays her hand on the bag at her side. "The lawyer called our house before I came here. He and the sanitary inspector are going to East Windsor tomorrow to decide how to clean up the place. They won't sell it until they know what's going to happen to her."

"Any chance she could go back there?"

"I doubt it. I'm not letting myself hope."

"How will you feel if they sell the house?"

Ellen closes her eyes. "I don't know. It's not really the same house as the one I loved. Still—I'll

198

be sad. I will." She opens her eyes again. "You know what's strange to think about?"

"What?"

"That whatever is left when she's gone will be mine."

"Too bad you don't have something now as a souvenir."

"I do have something," she says. "The letters from my father and me, and the purple ring, probably. I'm giving Eva my aquamarine to keep, so she'll have something from me. My mother says it's okay." She sits up. "What time is it?"

"You've got a couple more minutes. I have to be getting back to work myself."

"Ben?"

"Yeah?"

"Where's the line—between normal and crazy?"

"Oh, man." He locks his hands together. "This is my idea, okay? The line between normal and crazy . . . it's not a straight line—it's a lumpy circle. Some people are inside, some outside. Inside the circle, you're normal. You can go barefoot, wear rings in your ears, pull up mailboxes and still be on the inside. So long as you can laugh at yourself. But on the outside, you don't remember how to laugh, especially at yourself." He pauses. "Hey!" he says, nudging her. "Don't look so serious. What do *I* know?"

Ellen reaches for her bag. "It's time."

"What do you have in there?" Ben asks.

"The rings. Pictures from my mother's album, tissue paper for making flowers, one of Nonie's old hats—"

"What's that, in the paper bag?"

"Strawberries."

"Can I carry anything for you?"

"No, thanks, I've got it."

Ben's arm is around her waist as they walk along the flagstone path. At the end of it, before the line-up of ambulances, he pulls her close and kisses her. Her bag slips to the ground.

"I want to know everything about how it goes," Ben says as they separate. "Even if it's rough this time, you've got plenty of other chances. I'll come by after work, okay? So long!" Walking backward, he waves.

Ellen stays where she is until he crosses the street. The hospital, at sunset with lights in every window, looks less dreary than it does in the daytime. Slinging the bag over her shoulder, she goes in the main entrance and pushes the button for the elevator. And when it comes, she rises up on it to the sixth floor for her first visit with Eva in their new lives.

A NOTE ON THE TITLE

In *Hamlet* (Act III, Sc. i)
Ophelia is saddened when her beloved Hamlet,
whose words were once like music to her, now seems to be
"Like sweet bells jangled, out of tune and harsh. . . ."

R. F. B.

Robin Fidler Brancato
is one of today's most popular writers
of contemporary fiction for young adults.
Don't Sit Under the Apple Tree, Something Left to Lose,
Winning (1977 ALA Best Books for Young Adults),
Blinded by the Light (Literary Guild selection and
CBS Movie of the Week),
and *Come Alive at 505* (1980 ALA Best Books for Young Adults)
are all published by Knopf.

Ms. Brancato is a graduate of the University of Pennsylvania
and holds an M.A. from the City College of New York.
She has taught high school English for a number of years,
and lives with her husband, John, and their two teen-age sons
in Teaneck, New Jersey.